DANGER
ON THE
MOUNTAIN

CAROYLN LAROCHE

HOT TREE PUBLISHING

Marshall Brothers

Murder on the Mountain

Blue Ridge Murder

Danger on the Mountain

Defenders of Love

Witness Protection

Homeland Security

Border Patrol

DANGER ON THE MOUNTAIN

A MARSHALL BROTHERS NOVEL

CAROLYN LAROCHE

HOT TREE PUBLISHING

Danger on the Mountain © 2021 by Carolyn LaRoche

Danger on the Mountain is a work of fiction. All names, characters, events and places found therein are either from the author's imagination or used fictitiously. Any similarity to persons alive or dead, actual events, locations, or organizations is entirely coincidental and not intended by the author.

For information, contact the publisher, Hot Tree Publishing.

www.hottreepublishing.com

Editing: Hot Tree Editing

Cover Designer: BookSmith Design

E-book ISBN 978-1-922359-79-7

Paperback ISBN: 978-1-922359-80-3

*For my son Alex, and the entire
Class of 2021. No other graduating class
has ever had to do what you have accomplished
and you did with passion and style and grace.
I'm beyond proud of you, Alex.
You climbed the mountain,
slayed the demon and you're my hero for it.*

"I told you once the case was over, I wouldn't be your attorney anymore." Layla Evans walked out of the Virginia Beach Courthouse quickly, hoping the man following her would get the hint.

Unfortunately, he kept step with her, his insistence causing the little hairs on her neck to stand up and announce themselves. "I want to sue them, and the city, and I need a lawyer. You are my lawyer."

Layla stopped halfway down the wide stone steps and turned to look at him. "I'm a criminal defense attorney. My job for you is done. I don't do civil cases, and I definitely will not be representing you ever again."

His eyes turned hard. The angry expression scared her, but she held her ground. *Never let them see you scared.* Her law professor's words played over and over in her head as she held his stare with her own.

"You think I'm guilty, don't you?"

"It doesn't matter what I think, Jack. The jury acquitted you. I did my job. Now, if you'll excuse me, I have a meeting in thirty minutes." There was no meeting, but he didn't need to know that. She turned and started descending the steps again, but he grabbed her shoulder, squeezing so hard it hurt and stopping her in her tracks.

He leaned in and whispered next to her ear, his breath hot and moist, making her skin crawl. "You should be very proud. You managed to convince the jury I was innocent, even though your gut told you otherwise."

"Let me go." She shook her shoulder out of his grasp and took another step, freezing as a loud bang echoed through the air.

The thump of his body hitting the stone steps registered before she realized the bang was actually a gunshot.

Turning, Layla clapped a hand over her mouth. Blood ran freely from a wound in his chest, the life in his eyes disappearing rapidly.

Looking down, she could see blood spatter all

over her tan pants and the sleeve of her white blouse. Her stomach rolled as her knees buckled.

"Are you okay, Layla?" One of her colleagues stepped up beside her, grabbing her arm to keep her from rolling down the steps. He froze when he saw the man on the ground.

"Is that Jack Miles?" he asked, pointing at the body.

She nodded. "He wanted to sue the city and the family and wanted me to represent him."

"So you shot him?" He looked at her in disbelief.

A crowd had begun to gather.

"No! Of course not!" Layla rubbed her cheek, her fingers coming away covered in what she assumed was Jack's blood. "Oh my God."

"What happened?" someone asked.

"Someone shot the Kiddie Killer!" an older man said.

"I called 9-1-1!" someone else shouted.

The sheriff's deputies working inside the courthouse appeared and pushed the crowd back. One of them dropped to his knees and felt for a pulse, even though the large amount of blood on the ground told a solid story.

"He's dead," the deputy said. Looking up at Layla he asked, "Do you know what happened?"

"He was a former client of mine," she said. "He wanted me to represent him again. I was in the middle of telling him no when a shot rang out and he dropped."

"That's the Kiddie Killer," one of the other deputies said, scowling in Layla's direction. "And she's the one who got him off."

Resting her hands on her hips, Layla glared back. "Everyone has the right to a good defense. Innocent until proven guilty, remember?"

The deputy rolled his eyes. "Whatever helps you sleep at night, lady."

Several police cars and an ambulance roared up to the courthouse. Two cops jumped out and ran up the steps. "Is that who I think it is?" the female one asked her partner. "Good riddance, if you ask me."

"A man was just shot and killed six inches from me! This is no joke!" Layla balled her fists at her sides, ready to strike out at the next person who spoke.

"No it's not." The male officer squatted down and studied the wound. "This was pure karma. Someone wanted to be absolutely certain he'd never hurt another little girl again."

"He was acquitted!" Layla had no idea why she was defending the dirtbag she'd known was guilty.

Maybe for the sake of her reputation. More likely for the sake of her soul.

The medics made it to them, lugging a stretcher. "Let's get him out of here. I heard the news vans are on their way. This is the last thing that little girl's family needs to see now."

"Actually, it might be the best thing for them," one of the deputies said.

The female officer took Layla by the elbow and led her a few feet away. "I'm Officer Gonzalez. Can you tell me what happened here?"

Layla shook her head. "I didn't see anything. We were talking, I told him to leave me alone, and I started to walk away. The next thing I know, he's dead on the ground. This building is covered with cameras. I'm sure you'll be able to see the whole thing on film."

Officer Gonzalez took a few notes on an index card, then tucked it into her pocket. "I'll be in touch, Ms. Evans." The officer walked away, leaving her standing alone, covered in the blood of a killer and with no idea what to do next.

She stood there for another five minutes or so. The blood on her face smelled coppery, making her nauseous. No one seemed interested in her anymore, so she handed her business card to a detective she'd never met before and headed to the parking garage.

Layla climbed the steps slowly to the second level of the garage. The elevator hadn't worked in over a year, leaving her no choice. The tap of her heels on the concrete floor echoed throughout the space, matching the pounding of her heart as the full reality of what had just happened hit her hard as she slid in behind the wheel of her car. *What if that bullet had hit me? What if it were meant to hit me?*

Instead of returning to the office, Layla drove home. Pulling into the private parking garage, she found her assigned spot and parked. The large concrete wall in front of her reminded her of the courthouse. The tears fell as the adrenaline receded and her entire body shook. She'd been so proud when she bought the beachfront condo, her first big solo purchase since her fiancé had left. A dream come true that now felt like she'd broken a dozen laws to get there. The blood and tears of countless victims had funded the purchase. It was easy in the beginning, telling herself everyone was entitled to a good, solid defense. Layla believed in the system and juries to do the right thing. Unfortunately, they didn't always. She hadn't slept through a single night since that verdict had returned *not guilty*.

Her entire world had changed when the Kiddie Killer had been set free. He had been as guilty as the day is long but she'd done her job too well and he'd walked. Cecilia Owens's parents had received no closure, and Layla forgot how to sleep at night. She no longer believed the lies she'd told herself about right to counsel and everyone being entitled to a good defense. Her choices had far-reaching effects, the latest of which she'd witnessed that morning.

Grabbing her bag, Layla headed into the high-rise building. Stopping to grab her mail, she avoided eye contact with other residents and headed straight to the elevator. A minute later, she let herself into her condo and dumped everything on the kitchen counter. An official-looking letter slid to the floor. Layla bent over to pick it up and caught the name of an unfamiliar law practice in the return address.

"What now?" She sighed, tearing into the letter Maybe she was being sued. That would just be the icing on the damn cake. The formal letterhead gave pause to her agitation.

Dear Ms. Evans,

I am writing to inform you of the death of your father, Jacob Evans. He has named you as the only heir to his estate, to include personal property, funds and land. Please call our office at your earliest convenience to set up an appointment for the transfer of deeds and accounts.

Thank you,

Ramon Flores, ESQ

She ran her finger over the letterhead design of the smooth paper. Jacob Evans had died. The man listed on her birth certificate as her father had died and left her his estate. A father she barely remembered. A man who had walked out on his family and all his responsibilities when she could barely walk or talk.

Closing her eyes, she recalled the only memory she had of the man who'd donated half her genes: him getting into his blue pickup truck and driving away from her and Mama. From what she'd been told, she was three at the time. Mama caught him with another woman and kicked him out of the house. He'd gone across the state, bought a farm, and become a hermit. That was what her grandmother had told her. Mama refused to ever speak of him again after he left. Everything else she knew about Jacob she'd found through various internet searches.

Layla left the letter on the counter and went to the bathroom to take off her blood-splattered clothes. Stuffing them into the trash can, she reached in and turned on the water in the tub. She needed a shower in the worst way. Once the water had warmed, she stepped beneath the pounding spray. As she watched the red-tinted water run down the drain, tears rolled down her face. When she was done, she pulled on her robe and wrapped her long hair in a towel. There was no need to blow it dry as she had absolutely no intention of leaving her house that night. Or possibly for the next few months.

Picking up the letter and her cell phone on the way, Layla headed to the living room. After sitting on the couch with the paper in her lap for more than an hour, she finally picked up her cell phone and dialed her office.

The office manager, Shirley, answered on the second ring. "The law offices of Carmen and Carmen. How may I help you?"

"Shirley? It's Layla."

"Oh my goodness, dear heart! Are you okay? The bosses are worried about you!"

"I'm fine. I'm just calling to let you know I've had a death in the family, and I'm taking a few days off. Can you let the Carmens know, please?"

"A death in the family?" Shirley sounded

confused. "Were you related to that man who was shot?"

Layla shook her head, even though the other woman obviously couldn't see her. "Oh, no. That was Jack Miles. When I got home, I found out about this other thing. Can you keep this just between us, Shirley?"

She suddenly felt the need to tell someone, and her options were extremely limited.

"Of course I can, dear heart." Shirley had lowered her voice to a conspiratorial whisper.

Layla exhaled, trying to slow her racing heart. "My father died."

There was a long pause. "Your father? I didn't realize—"

"I never really knew him. He left when I was three," she interrupted. "I got a letter today from his attorney. Apparently he left me everything in his will."

"Oh." The other woman let out a long breath of air. "Maybe he was crazy rich and you're about to become disgustingly wealthy."

Layla chuckled. "I don't think so, Shirley."

"Well, you take care of yourself. After what happened today, a couple days out of town might be good for you." Shirley hung up before she could respond.

That settled, she dialed the number of the law office of Ramon Flores.

"How can I help you today?" The upbeat, friendly voice caught her a little off guard.

"I, um… I received a letter today saying I should call and set up an appointment. My name is Layla Evans."

"Ms. Evans! We've been waiting for your call. Can you meet Mr. Flores tomorrow afternoon?"

The next day? Reality hit her hard.

"Tomorrow? Um—"

"I can schedule you for one in the afternoon, right after lunch. That will give you plenty of time to drive to Staunton from Virginia Beach."

Wow, they'd done their homework.

"Well, okay, then. I suppose I could do tomorrow. But—"

"Excellent! I've got you marked down on the schedule. Be sure to bring your picture identification, Social Security card, and birth certificate if you have it."

Birth certificate? Picture identification? "Okay."

"Excellent! See you tomorrow, then." The receptionist disconnected without giving Layla an opportunity to disagree.

She dug out her birth certificate and Social Security card, setting them by her purse. Exhausted, she fell into bed and slept nearly ten minutes past her alarm.

———

BEN MARSHALL HAD SO MANY OTHER THINGS HE could be doing. The stiff, uncomfortable suit felt like a straitjacket, and the tie might as well have been a noose around his neck. He definitely preferred a pair of jeans and a long-sleeved T-shirt. The sooner he could get back to his farm, the better.

Large raindrops slapped against the windshield as he drove down the mountain. The letter he'd received from the only law office in town had confused him. Parking his truck in the closest available spot to the door, he turned off the engine and gave himself a moment to mentally prepare. After everything that had happened in recent years, appearing anywhere in a public place increased his anxiety to DEFCON levels. It took all his self-control not to turn that truck back around and go home. Nothing that old man Evans could have left him would be worth the stress of people seeing him. Lauren had definitely made that clear.

Jogging through the rain, he made it to the large glass doors and walked into the building. An elevator to his right was just opening for an older woman who stood waiting, foot tapping incessantly He followed her in and moved to the corner, his back to the wall. She paid him no attention at all, getting off one floor before his destination.

The attorney's office was smaller than he'd expected. Ben shifted in his chair for about the hundredth time since being told by the receptionist to have a seat.

His appointment had been at one. It was now ten past. One thing Ben's military personality had no tolerance for was lateness. He considered leaving.

A moment later a sexy brunette with curves for miles stepped out of an office. "Mr. Flores will see you now."

The lady next to him stood up at the same time he did.

Ben paused. "Which of us did you mean?"

The woman shrugged. "Both of you."

He glanced at the lady in the black dress and heels, then back at the brunette. "Are you sure?'

"Yes, sir." The secretary settled behind her desk,

blowing a bubble with some chewing gum. "Benjamin Marshall, meet Layla Evans. Now go on inside please. Mr. Flores is waiting."

Ben motioned to Ms. Evans to go ahead first. She strode to the office, looking more than a little annoyed, and pulled the door open.

"Mr. Flores?" she asked as they entered the room.

A tall, well-built man with salt-and-pepper hair and a welcoming smile stood up behind his desk.

"Come in. Both of you." He motioned to two chairs. "Have a seat, please."

"Good afternoon." The woman stepped forward, hand extended to the attorney. Her dress hugged her curves as though it had been made just for her. "I'm Layla Evans."

The attorney accepted her hand, holding it between both of his. "I am so very sorry for your loss."

She flipped her long chestnut-colored hair over her shoulder. "Don't be. I never even knew the man."

Mr. Flores frowned slightly. "I'm sorry to hear that." He extended a hand to Ben. "Thank you for joining us, Mr. Marshall."

Ben grunted and lowered himself into a chair. "I'm not sure why I'm here. I hardly knew the man."

Layla sat in the chair beside him, and Mr. Flores settled back into his desk chair.

"Mr. Evans had great respect for you and your service to our country. Not to mention the times you assisted him on his land. He wanted to show his appreciation."

Ben frowned. "He doesn't owe me anything. I was just being neighborly is all."

"Still, he was adamant that you received this." He handed a brown paper package to Ben, who set it on his lap.

It had a little weight to it, which surprised him. "Do you know what it is?"

The attorney nodded. "His antique Colt revolver you had admired."

Ben shook his head. "That's much too generous. I can't accept it."

"And deny a dead man his final wishes?" Mr. Flores smiled. "It's in the will, Mr. Marshall. He felt you'd earned it for your sacrifices for our country."

Layla gave him a look he couldn't quite identify.

"Thank you. I appreciate it very much."

Mr. Flores handed a file and an envelope to Layla. "This is your father's will. In it he names you to receive everything else. The envelope contains bank books and statements, keys to the property and vehicles, and a few other important documents. If you could sign a few papers for me, I can get to work on transferring the deeds and monies to you."

Layla frowned, setting the items on the desk in front of her. "Why would a man I haven't seen since I was three years old leave me anything?"

The attorney folded his hands on his desk and leaned toward her, his expression serious. "I knew your father fairly well, Layla. His biggest regret in life was abandoning you."

"Oh, boo-hoo. I feel so sad for him." She didn't even try to cover her sarcasm as she pushed the envelope back across the desk. "I don't want—or need—anything from him."

Ben bit back a laugh. He kinda liked this woman.

Ramon pushed the envelope back to her. "Please, Layla. Let him make it up to you. You'll be quite surprised by his land. It's beautiful. He built most of the home himself, and the view is amazing."

"If it's truly all that, I should make a good bit of money off it when I sell it all, then." Layla leaned toward the desk. "Show me where to sign. The sooner I sell this stuff, the sooner I can be rid of that man for good."

Mr. Flores frowned. Ben watched as the slight quiver in her jaw belied the firm set to her shoulders. Ms. Layla Evans had daddy issues and a boat-load of baggage.

Of course, he was one to talk.

He had more than his fair share of baggage. Enough to keep him away from his mother and his five brothers—and forget about falling in love ever again. Nope. He liked the solitude of his life. Having Layla around, for any length of time, could upset that balance, and he had no interest in that. With any luck, she'd send a realtor to handle the sale and he wouldn't have to deal with the slight interest she'd piqued in him.

"Do you need me to sign anything, sir?" Ben asked the lawyer.

"No. You're good to go, Mr. Marshall. Thank you for coming by today."

"Thank you, sir." Ben rose and carried his package out of the office. As he stepped into the elevator, the thought occurred to him that he should have offered to show Layla the way to her father's land.

No. It was better to not encourage any interaction between them. The kind of, sort of attraction he felt for the woman angrily signing paperwork in the attorney's office would be nothing but trouble for him. He knew that with every cell of his being.

CHAPTER TWO

LAYLA SAT BACK ON THE LITTLE WOOD STOOL AND stared at the cow that stood in front of her. After six months of trying, she hadn't gotten any better at this particular chore. In fact, she despised it. Leaning forward, she attempted to milk the beast once more.

"The next time I decide to try to run a ranch, just shoot me." The cow grunted and kicked the bucket over, spilling what little milk she *had* gotten all over her jeans. She kicked the metal bucket across the stall, where it landed in a nasty pile of straw and manure. "Ugh! I knew I should have sold this place!"

Warm, chocolate brown eyes watched her with pity as Chloe, one of the two dairy cows she'd inherited, snorted softly. Even the cow knew how pathetic she was. When she'd first met with the attorney, she'd been hell bent on ditching this property and continuing on with her life. She should have stuck with the original plan. Not that she could have stayed in her job any longer either.

"I was stuck between a rock and a hard place, Chloe." She patted the animal on the shoulder. "You understand, don't you?"

Chloe let out a little grunt and seemed to nod her head.

Layla grabbed the bucket, sat back down on the rickety little stool, and gave one of the udders a good squeeze like she'd seen on the internet. Milk hit the side of the bucket, sprayed in her face, and ran down the front of her shirt.

"That's it, I'm done." She rose from the stool and backed out of the stall. "Come on, Chloe, let's get you out in the pasture with Zoe. You two gals can soak up a little sunshine while I figure out how I ended up here."

Chloe let out another grunt as Layla slowly led her toward the barn door.

Leaving her job as a criminal defense attorney with a prominent law firm in Virginia Beach had seemed like a really good idea when she did it. She was exhausted, burnt out really, from the evils of humankind. Spending her days with cows and horses sounded so much better. Excellent therapy for a stressed and injured soul. Except she didn't know a damned thing about raising cattle, milking a cow, or riding a ranch horse. Ten years of riding lessons, prancing around an arena, and dressing in fancy riding gear hadn't prepared her in the least for the wild nature of the horses at her new home.

"Let's move it, girl. We're burning daylight here!" At least she had the lingo down. Hours of watching online videos on how to care for ranch animals had taught her that.

Layla laughed at the ridiculousness of it all.

Once she managed to get the huge animal out into the pasture with her calf, she had to saddle up the one horse she could pretty much handle and ride the fence line. One of the videos said if she didn't want her cattle to escape, she had to check for breaks in the fencing. He called it riding the fence.

Chloe finally sauntered out into the sunlight and immediately started grazing along the fresh spring grasses that were finally poking through the old hay Layla spread during the winter months. It took longer than it should have to saddle up Domino, the largest of the horses in the stable. Country Cattle Man, her favorite video host, made riding the fence look like a walk in the park, so Layla figured it would be like one of those mud runs she'd done a couple summers ago—sloppy, sweaty, and dirty but done by the end of the day.

Two hundred and fifty acres of grazing lands in the foothills of the Blue Ridge Mountains had replaced her beachfront condo. No more briefs, motions, or subpoenas. Her primary income source had now become a midsize herd of Angus beef cattle. As soon as she figured out what she was supposed to do with them and when. Hopefully, Country Cattle Man had a video on that too.

A simple fence of wood posts and barbed wire snaked its way around through brush and fields, even crossing the small stream she'd discovered running through one back corner of the property. She didn't have a clue about handling cattle, so she had a couple hired hands who tended to most of that business. They came three or four times a week and did what needed doing. She'd saved her property's perimeter fence for herself though.

If she wanted to be a rancher, then she had to act like one.

Scrambling astride her huge mount, Layla urged the beast forward with a gentle nudge from her heels and a click of her tongue, just like Country Cattle Man did with his horse. Domino just stood where he was. Some days he did exactly what she wanted and others… well, he could be as stubborn as she was.

"Come on, Dom, let's go!" Frustrated, she yanked the reins, muttered a curse, and kicked harder. Domino strode toward the barn door. Apparently the animal liked to be cursed at. That made her wonder about her father for the hundredth or so time since moving to the ranch.

Once they stepped outside the barn, Domino took off. Layla held on to the reins as tight as she could. Domino always ran like his tail was on fire when they first left the barn, so she just held on and waited. As was his fashion, Domino slowed to a decent trot as they crossed the field and headed toward the fence. She got the feeling that the horse had ridden the fences more than a few times in his day.

A few hours later, as the stream came into view, Layla felt pretty confident. They were more than halfway through the day and the fence had proven sturdy so far. She stopped the horse at the edge of the water so he could take a drink. As Domino did his thing, Layla downed half a bottle of water herself, then pulled her cell phone out to check the time.

Movement on the other side of the barbed wire

caught her eye. Bright red shone through the green of the trees and brush. She felt for the shotgun she'd gotten used to taking with her on rides, slung down by the saddle.

The brush moved. A branch snapped.

Layla tried to turn Domino away from the water, but the stubborn beast refused to move. She tugged at the shotgun, but her shaking hands fumbled with the sling.

"Let's move, Domino!" She tried to get the horse going, but still he ignored her. Panicked, she yanked at the shotgun, finally setting it free, and raised it to her shoulder.

"Who's there?" she demanded, hoping the shake in her voice was only audible to her.

Something shot out of the brush, running at Domino. The horse startled, rearing up on his hind legs.

Layla's body flew through the air, landing on the grassy embankment just as the world went black.

"SON OF A BITCH!" BEN MARSHALL DROPPED THE rabbit he was holding by the legs and sprinted to where the woman lay in a pile of brush.

A tiny stream of blood trickled from a gash on her forehead. Ben grabbed the first aid kit from his backpack and tore open a pack of gauze, pressing it gently to the wound on her face. She stirred slightly but didn't wake up. He looked around for her horse, but the animal was long gone.

"Miss? Miss, can you hear me?" He jostled her ever so slightly. Something about her felt familiar.

"Mmm…." She moaned and tried to roll over.

"No! Don't move." Ben placed a hand on her shoulder to keep her from rolling.

"What happened?" Her words came out on a breathy moan. "Who… who are you?"

"Name's Ben Marshall, and I'm the guy who's gonna get you help."

"I don't need help. I just need to get out of here." She pulled herself up into a sitting position, ignoring his command to stay still.

"You really should get checked out. You hit your head on the fall. There could be internal injuries." Ben reached for her arm to help her up, but the woman scooted out of his reach.

"I'm fine. I just need to get home. Where's Domino?" She looked around. The movement forced the trickle of blood on her forehead into her eye. "I'm bleeding."

Ben reached out again, holding the gauze. "Here. Use this to put pressure on it."

Their fingers grazed as she accepted his offering. The contact was brief but electrified.

You've been alone way too long.

Two years basically living in isolation from most humans would make any man hungry for a little close physical contact of the female kind.

He watched as she applied the gauze to her wound. Her shoulder-length brown curls were tangled with a twig and a couple leaves. She watched him warily with green hazel eyes surrounded by eyelashes that never needed to see a drop of mascara, they were so long and full.

Ignoring the fact that he'd just noticed all that, Ben moved toward the woman slowly, like he would approach a spooked horse. She had that same look of fear he'd seen on a hundred soldiers after an IED exploded. He knew she would have already taken off through the trees if she weren't still reeling from her spill.

"You really should get to a hospital. You could have a concussion."

"I'm fine. Just a little sore," she snapped, backing a little farther away from him.

"I'm not going to hurt you. You know that, right?"

People were always afraid of him. He couldn't blame them; his disfigured body was nothing to look at, not even taking into account the emotional scars he carried with him.

She nodded but didn't look convinced, although he gave her props for trying to

appear confident. "I... I know. I just need to find my horse." She glanced around as if to make her point.

"Your horse took off. Probably back at the barn by now, grazing on the fresh grass and wondering what's taking you so long to catch up. He'll expect a full brushing when you return." Ben offered her a smile, a lot more crooked and uneven than it used to be thanks to one very sharp blade and a pissed-off enemy soldier.

Surprisingly, she smiled back. Sort of. "I guess I have quite a long walk back."

Suddenly he remembered where he'd met her before. "You the lady who took over the Evans ranch?"

"Why?" She stiffened and her eyes narrowed with instant distrust as she studied him.

He motioned to her, then himself. "We met at the attorney's office."

Taking a moment to study him, she finally

nodded. "Oh, right. You look… different than you did there."

"I hate wearing suits. Mama would have had my hide if I'd shown up dressed like this though."

She chuckled a little. "You're a grown man. You still worry about what your mother thinks?"

"You aren't?" He opened his bag and pulled out a couple bottles of water and two protein bars. "Southern Mamas have spies everywhere." He laughed, the sound a little rusty to his ears. "I'd never hear the end of how I wasn't raised in a barn, blah, blah, blah."

"My parents are from Massachusetts. In Boston they kick you out of the nest and see if you can fly before they join a country club and basically forget they have a kid." She frowned. "I guess I should say my mother and my stepfather. That man couldn't wait for me grow up and move out."

"Ah, so you're a Yankee, then." He offered her a bottle of water and one of the bars. "Are you thirsty? Hungry? I didn't expect to have company, so it's nothing fancy, but you're welcome to it."

"Thank you." She frowned as she accepted his offerings. "You say that like it's an insult."

"Say what?"

Layla took a long swallow of water before

answering. "That I'm a Yankee. I'm nothing like my parents."

"Sorry. Certainly didn't mean it that way." He crouched down with his back against a tree. Ben never let his back go unguarded. He'd definitely learned that the hard way.

"Besides, my mom died a few years ago, so there's that."

Ben studied a rock in the dirt in front of him. "I'm real sorry to hear that."

She took a long drink of water. "That's so good. Thanks again. Domino took off with my pack. I was planning lunch here by the stream before… before you showed up and…."

"And spooked your horse out from under you?"

"Something like that." This smile was bigger but still didn't quite reach her eyes. She took another sip of water.

Her lips were damp and glossy. Something deep in his gut churned. "You're welcome. We really should get you home. I've got my horse just over the stream. I'll grab him and give you a ride back."

"Hey, what happened to the fencing that went over the stream?" she asked, ignoring everything he just said.

"I removed it."

"Why? That's my property. You can't do that." She motioned toward the stream.

He shrugged. "It was catching storm debris and backing up the flow."

"You still shouldn't have touched it. It's on my property."

Ben stepped over so he could look her right in the eye. "And your property would have flooded after a heavy rain, washing away a lot more of your fence. Everyone knows you don't put a fence in running water. Why would you have done that?"

She pursed her lips and glared at him. "Because."

It took all his self-control not to laugh. He had a feeling that would have been a very bad move, but she had really begun to irritate him. "Because? That's your reason?"

"I thought the fence had come down, so I had one of my ranch hands repair it."

"And the fool went and did it? He should have known better."

Hands on her hips, she scowled. "He did what I asked him to because *he* works for *me*."

Ben shook his head, slowly and deliberately. "I don't know who you think you are, but you're sure no farm girl or cattle rancher. Just look at you. Are you wearing *designer* cowboy boots?"

"I *like* these boots!" she snapped.

"They're completely impractical. And further proof that you know absolutely nothing about running a ranch. Whoever put that fence up for you was an idiot. You defending it makes you a bigger idiot." He tossed his first aid kit back in his pack and zipped it up. Let her find her own way home. He didn't need this sort of aggravation in his life.

She followed him as he tried to walk away. "I am not an idiot! How dare you! No wonder you wander out here in the woods alone. No one could put up with your nasty attitude! Just where do you get off anyway, telling me who and what I am?"

His nasty attitude? That was it? That was the reason she thought he hid out on his own ranch?

"Look, lady—"

"The name's Layla! Don't call me '*lady*.'" She actually stomped her foot for emphasis, and it took all his composure to not dissolve in laughter.

"Okay, *Layla*, I'm sorry you're angry about the fence, but it had to be done. If that backed up, it could cause a flood on your property and cut off water to mine. I didn't know you were living here now. I figured Evans would have wanted me to fix the problem. That's what ranchers do for each other."

"Oh." A crimson flush rose slowly out of the neckline of her long-sleeved shirt, traveling up her neck and over her smooth features.

The blush intrigued him, making him want to spend more time with her and find other ways to make it happen. That annoyed him considerably. Ben liked his solitude. How dare this gorgeous woman ride in on a horse way too big for her and destroy his quiet life?

He let out a low whistle and waited until his horse, Sam, appeared through the brush. "I'm sorry about the fence. Make sure you get someone to look at that cut on your head." He felt her eyes on him as he splashed through the water and climbed in the saddle Sam wore.

"You're just going to leave?" she called after him as he turned Sam around and started making their way back toward home.

"It was nice to meet you again, Layla!" he called over his shoulder.

Actually, it was not nice at all. She had him all confused with her hot-and-cold behavior. And the way his body responded to hers threatened his care-fully carved-out existence. He didn't need that in his life. Nope. What he needed was a cold shower and a beer. Maybe a thick steak on the grill and one of those potatoes he'd pulled out of the ground in his garden. Yup, that was all he needed—steak, potatoes, and beer. And to forget he'd ever met the feisty Layla. Nothing good could come of it. Even if they one day learned to get along and maybe she wasn't so bothered by the scar on his face. Experience told him there was no way she could look past the rest of what those monsters had done to him.

He'd made it about a hundred feet into the woods when he started to feel guilty. He'd be a monster if he made that woman find her way back in the dark —and it would be dark long before she made it home.

"What the hell," he muttered as he pulled up on the reins. "Come on, Sam. Let's go get her."

Sam snorted agreement and turned back toward where Layla had last been. As they broke through the brush by the stream, Ben caught sight of her picking her way slowly and tediously along the embankment. His gaze wandered over her figure and the way those jeans fit her curves perfectly, as though they were made just for her. Perhaps there was something to be said for designer fashion after all.

Get your head on straight, man. You do not need that in your life right now.

His brain knew what was up. But the rest of him had no interest in paying attention. As his internal battle waged, he pushed Sam to pick up the pace until they were right beside her. The little trail was barely wide enough to accommodate them both, so he let her get a couple steps ahead. She refused to look up at him.

"Come on, Layla, let Sam and me give you a ride home."

"I'm fine, thanks," she replied without making eye contact.

"It's a long way back, and you're in no condition —" Good Lord, he'd just made it sound like she was pregnant or something. *Smooth, Marshall. Very smooth.*

"Why don't you go on back to your cave or rock or wherever it is you live? I've got a long way to go, and I don't have time to deal with you."

He pulled Sam to a stop and jumped down. Leading the horse by the reins, he fell into step beside her. "I'm sorry. I can come across as a real ass sometimes."

She gave him a sideways glance. "I bet you're a real riot at parties and weddings."

Layla had spunk. And a sense of humor. Two pluses in his book.

"I said I was sorry. I'm not what you would call a social guy. I'm a little rusty on how to interact with the general public."

"Yeah, well, I'm not a fan of the general public either. Or guys who act like asses."

Try as he might not to, he'd really started to like Layla.

"Your father never mentioned that he had a daughter."

"Maybe he forgot. It'd been like thirty years since we saw each other." The hurt in her voice hit him in the heart.

"I'm sorry, Layla. That must have been rough."

"Let's just say the men in my life have left a lot to be desired." Finally, she looked over at him. "Go home, Ben. I'm fine."

Before he could reply, her boot hit a loose stone, turning her ankle and sending her to the ground. "Ouch!"

"Okay, Layla Evans, no more arguing. Sam insists." Without another word, he grabbed her at the waist with both hands and lifted her into the saddle. Then Ben climbed up and settled behind her, his arms wrapping around her.

Touching her turned up the heat in his blood almost instantly. His body felt rigid as her back pressed against his chest. In his mind, she could feel every scar across his body—even though he logically knew she couldn't. He kept expecting her to push him away in revulsion. But she didn't. In fact, he kind of felt her relax against his chest, and that cranked up the volume of the pulse sounding in his ears.

For the first time in over a year, Ben actually felt a little bit happy.

CHAPTER THREE

So much for being a strong, independent woman.

Domino obviously had no allegiance to her, running off and leaving her in a heap on the ground like he did. What about those horses on television who stayed by their masters until their dying breath? Now she had to accept help, and that was the last thing she wanted—a stranger entering her safe domain.

Even if that stranger was steaming hot and had a voice as smooth as Tennessee whiskey, despite the huge chip he carried on his shoulder.

They rode in complete silence as the sun set and the sounds of night began to fill in around them. As dusk moved in, she became more grateful that Ben had insisted on giving her a ride home. She wasn't as familiar with the ranch as he seemed to be. She'd have gotten lost for sure.

"Did you know him well?" The question came out before she had a chance to think about it.

Ben shrugged. She could feel the movement against her back. "Not really. Folks 'round here help each other occasionally. You get neighborly, but everyone is too busy making a living to get friendly."

"He liked you well enough to leave you something in his will." They hit a bumpy area. The extra movement caused Ben to hold her a bit tighter as he worked the reins.

"It wasn't much of anything. Just a token from one soldier to another."

"Oh." She hadn't known her father had been in the military. "Have you been a rancher all your life? I mean, except for the time you were in the service?"

His laugh was humorless. "Not sure I'd call myself a rancher, and no. Just a few years."

"What brought you here, then? Does your family live here?"

Ben stiffened against her. He was silent for so long, she thought he wouldn't answer. Just when Layla decided he wasn't going to reply, he spoke. "I needed a change of pace."

Well, they had that in common.

"Me too," she replied.

They went back to being silent as Ben's horse crested the last rise before her barn came into view. Even from there she could see that all the lights inside the building were on and the big front doors were banging in the evening breeze.

"Stop." She put her hand on Ben's without thinking. The jolt of pure electricity that passed through their touch nearly threw her from her second horse of the day.

Ben drew the horse to a stop. "What's wrong?" He sounded more than a little annoyed.

"The barn. Something's wrong. The lights are on and the doors are open."

"So? Your ranch hands are probably doing the evening chores."

Layla shook her head. "No. This is their day off. They only come during the week."

"Oh." Ben sucked in a breath. "Could you have forgotten to close the doors when you left this morning?"

"Maybe that's possible, but I definitely didn't leave the lights on like that. It was the middle of the morning. I didn't need any with the doors open."

Ben tightened his grip on the reins and urged the horse to a trot. When they got about five hundred feet from the barn, he pulled the horse to a stop and lowered himself to the ground. Pulling a pistol from his saddlebag, he clicked the safety off.

"Stay here." It was a command, not a request. Obviously Ben was used to being in charge with his military background, but he didn't have the right to tell her what to do on her own property. She dropped down to the ground, trying not to wince as her sore body made contact, and followed him.

"I told you to stay here."

"You can't tell me what to do. This is my barn."

He glared at her. "Have you always been so difficult?"

She glared back. "Anyone who doesn't do what you say is 'difficult'?"

He didn't say anything, but she could he really wanted to. Layla sighed. "This is my home. I need to be able to protect it, same as you with your place."

Ben looked at her for a long moment, then gave a single nod. "Fine. But stay behind me. I don't want to worry about you getting shot or something."

Layla did as she was told, but only because she agreed with Ben. She still carried her shotgun but didn't really trust herself to hit an actual target yet. It was more like a security blanket for her than an actual weapon of protection. Ben didn't need to know that though. He looked plenty nervous enough when she'd aimed it at him earlier. That was all she needed. Of course, it didn't stop her from being happy that he was bigger, stronger, and, judging by the way he held that weapon, way more experienced.

They inched forward through the twilight. Ben moved silently, his gaze steady and focused. He was a predator, and whatever was in that barn was his unsuspecting prey.

When they reached the back wall of the structure, Ben crouched below one of the open shutters. No sound came from inside. Chloe and Zoe were still grazing, and Domino wandered around behind the house snacking on grass.

Slowly, Ben rose and peered into the opening from one corner. After a second he let out a low whistle and stood up. Tucking the gun in the back of his waistband, he strode toward the front of the barn.

Racing to catch up with him, Layla was out of breath when she pulled up in front of the open building and looked inside.

"What the hell happened to my barn?"

The place was a mess. Hay bales had been sliced open and tossed everywhere. Ropes, saddles, and bridles were strewn across the floor, and every piece of equipment that had hung neatly from pegs on the wall had been taken down and thrown into stalls with the other two horses.

"Looks like you had a visitor."

"Gee, you think?" Layla pushed past him.

"Wait! They could still be in there!" Ben called after her, but she ignored him.

Heavy footsteps sounded and then strong arms wrapped around her, taking them both to the ground as two gunshots rang out. A little whistling noise passed by her head just before a piece of one of the stalls blew up beside them.

"Someone is shooting at us!" Layla tried to jump up and run, but Ben held tight.

"Shh!" He clamped a hand lightly over her mouth. "Don't talk, and hold still," he whispered by her ear.

Layla nodded. She watched as Ben pulled himself up into a crouch, holding his gun in front of him, and slowly moved around so he could see the door on the far side of the building.

Ben disappeared from her sight for a few minutes, then returned, closing and latching the door behind him. "It's all clear, Layla."

She stood up and started taking stock of the damage. So far it just looked like someone made a mess. No real destruction other than the hay all over the place. And the destroyed board on the stall beside her.

Ben quickly crossed the space between them, his expression hard and unforgiving.

"You're an idiot."

"What?" Layla asked, still distracted by the mess.

"I said you're an idiot."

"Where do you get off calling me names?" she snapped.

"You're tactically unsound. You went tearing off into this place without a clue as to whether it was safe or not. People like you are a liability to the mission."

"The mission? What mission?" Layla demanded, balling her hands into fists and willing the threatening tears to hold off. She refused to cry in front of that man. "This is my *home*! Someone came in here and destroyed my stuff. And then they tried to shoot me!" The tears she had fought so hard to hold back every day since the shooting on the courthouse steps ran down her cheeks as all the frustration she'd been ignoring poured from her eyes.

Ben just stood there looking at her, his eyes hard but not entirely unfeeling.

Layla turned her back to him and wiped at her eyes. "Why don't you just go now? I have a lot of cleaning up to do. Thank you for bringing me home." She grabbed a rake and started pushing the straw around, ignoring him as he walked out. She didn't need him hanging around anyway.

Layla kicked at a saddle that was tossed in the middle of the floor. Why would anyone do this to her? She didn't even know anyone in town. Maybe her father had enemies she wasn't aware of. But if he had enemies, wouldn't they know he'd died?

It was probably just a bunch of kids causing trouble.

Sure. Kids. Teenagers were always getting into something. She was the new girl in town, and they were trying to let her know she wasn't welcome.

But firing a gun at her?

That was no teenage prank.

Layla knew she didn't belong there any more now than she did when she moved in. None of that mattered though. Her old life no longer existed. She had to make this one work.

The tears started up again, pissing her off. She was *not* used to feeling so helpless. Back in Virginia Beach, *she* made people cry, not the other way around.

"Damn it all to hell," she muttered as she dropped to an undamaged hay bale and lowered her head into her hands.

BEN WALKED OUT OF THE BARN WITHOUT SAYING A word. If she wanted him gone, then gone he would be. The last thing he needed was another whiny woman in his life. Layla Evans didn't really strike him as a whiny woman though. She exuded a vibe of self-confidence and security that Lauren had lacked.

The thought of his ex-fiancée brought on a fresh layer of annoyance. Lauren and Layla were absolutely nothing alike. He could tell that already. Although he had no idea why he cared.

Okay, so maybe he did. That steak and beer idea from earlier had really begun to sound good—this time though, he envisioned the entire six-pack as an hors d'oeuvre.

When he stepped outside the circle of light from the barn door, he stopped to tie the laces on his boot. As he righted himself, Ben caught sight of Layla sitting on a hay bale looking about as lost as he'd ever seen a person. The natural instinct to help, to fix whatever ailed her, overwhelmed his desire to get out of there.

"Aw, hell." He turned and walked back to the barn. Standing in the doorway, he offered up a half smile. "Come on, let's clean this place up."

Layla looked up at him, her eyes tired and red rimmed from crying. "Go away, Ben. I don't need your pity. Even an idiot can work a rake."

He dug the toe of his boot into some hay. "Yeah, about that. Sorry. I shouldn't have called you an idiot."

Layla stood up and grabbed a rake. "Whatever. Just go ahead home to your life and leave me to figure out mine." She started clearing the straw with a vengeance. He watched for a full minute before grabbing a rake and joining her. She glanced at him but didn't say anything.

Layla brushed by him, grabbing saddles and bridles and miscellaneous other items. He just kept raking and trying to figure out this major bump in his regular routine.

"What's your last name again, Ben?"

Ben went into one of the stalls and started gathering tools. Layla worked her way over to the stall entrance. He tossed two pitchforks and a broom on his shoulder.

Layla stepped forward, her eyes on Ben. "You know—"

Her words were lost as she suddenly lunged toward him when her foot caught on a stray rake. They tumbled together, landing in a heap on the barn floor, Layla sprawled across his body, her face mere inches from his.

If anyone asked him later, there would be no way he could explain what he did next. Maybe it was the breathless way she looked at him from under long, partially lowered eyelashes and how perfect her soft curves felt across his aching, lonely body. Whatever possessed him to kiss her, Ben couldn't say. When he pulled her in close, the feel of her lips on his sent sparks of energy to every cell in his body like nothing he'd ever experienced before. With that contact, he forgot about Lauren breaking his heart. All the self-loathing he'd nurtured so well over the past months became a distant memory. Parts of his body that had gone dormant were suddenly so alive it overwhelmed him. The scars on his body disappeared from his mind.

He ran his tongue over her lips tentatively, wondering if she would grant him access to deepen the kiss or if she would suddenly jump up and run from him. When Layla responded by parting her lips with a soft little moan, he felt like he'd just won the lottery. It was akin to heaven on earth. Food for the starving man he'd become. She was soft and warm and just felt so damned good against his tense muscles and aching soul. All the months of denying that he needed human contact dissipated. Layla's body felt perfect against his. Like she'd been made just for him.

He fisted his hands in the material of her shirt, pulling it from the waist of her jeans. Without any thought as to what he was doing, Ben slid his fingertips across the soft skin of her lower back. His heart banged around inside his chest, trying to keep up with the pulse racing in his ears and the blood heating in his veins. Her silky-smooth skin begged him to seek more, and he wasn't about to disappoint.

Layla let her fingers roam up his arms, across his shirt-covered chest. Everywhere she touched branded him with reminders that he'd been alone for so long. He craved the feeling of a woman again, more than even he had realized.

Until her fingers moved from his shoulder to his cheek. As she began to gently trace the raised area along his jaw, Ben's body shut down. All the intense feelings suddenly died. The fireworks that had been going off inside him disappeared abruptly. He pushed her off him and jumped to his feet.

Layla looked up at him from the pile of straw like an injured doe, big green eyes brimming with moisture and surprise.

"I'm sorry," she whispered. "I don't know what

happened. I think I just got caught up in the moment... and I've been so alone. I shouldn't have kissed you."

She shouldn't have kissed *him*? He wasn't sure she had that right. He knew for a fact, though, that he'd wanted it more than he wanted life itself.

"You didn't do anything wrong. I was totally out of line."

"No." Layla shook her head. "It's okay. It's my fault. I tripped and fell."

"It takes two to tango, as my mother would say." He leaned down and offered her a hand, pulling her to her feet. She stumbled a little, forcing his arms to wrap around her once more to keep her on her feet. It wasn't something he wanted to like, but oh, how he did.

That nagging little voice that liked to constantly remind him he was no longer right for any woman showed up again.

"I'm not what you think I am," he blurted as they stood there together.

Layla frowned. "Just what do I think you are?"

"Um, I don't know." He could feel the heat rising in his face. He looked away.

She pressed her fingertips lightly to his cheek and turned him to look at her. "You certainly presume to know what's in my head, so why don't you share it with me?"

He resisted the urge to jump away as her fingers brushed over the scar he hated so much. "I'm just saying—"

"I think you're a nice man who feels it's his duty to help someone in distress, even when you want to walk away. I think you've condemned yourself to a life of being alone, for reasons I cannot begin to know, but that you're as lonely as I am."

Was he really such an open book?

"There are things about me—" He sighed as his shoulders slumped. "I shouldn't have let that happen. I'm sorry."

Layla reached up and ran one finger along the edge of the scar on his face, tracing the entire length. He resisted the urge to jerk away. Her touch was gentle, her expression soft. God, he could really get used to her touch.

"Is this one of those things?" she asked.

One of many. He closed his eyes, trying to not to let the emotion show. The one she touched was the only scar he couldn't cover with his clothing. When she started a second exploration of his face, he stepped back. He couldn't bear to repulse another woman the way he had Lauren. "I should really get going. Let's lock this place up, and I'll clear your house before I leave."

Back to business. Back to doing what he knew best: being alone.

She nodded and stepped away to hang up the rake she'd dropped when they took their tumble.

Ben watched her move, sadness weighing down on him. This night was the first time since Lauren had tossed her engagement ring in his face that he'd allowed himself to enjoy anything.

Layla finished hanging the rest of the tools and headed toward the door. Ben followed, Lauren's parting words ringing in his mind. *"You're broken, Ben, and no one will ever be able to fix you."*

CHAPTER FOUR

"THANK YOU." HE'D FINISHED HELPING HER CHECK HER house, and as far as they could tell, nothing had been disturbed. They now stood in the dirt drive between the house and the barn.

"No thanks necessary. It was sort of my fault anyway," Ben replied, not making eye contact. Things had definitely gotten weird since the kiss in the barn. Not that it shouldn't have. She'd made a complete fool of herself.

Layla shrugged. "You had nothing to do with it."

"Not the barn. But I did spook your horse." He kicked a rock with his boot. "I suppose it's best I be on my way. My place is the next one up the road on the left if you ever need anything."

"Okay." She gave him a small smile, hoping the darkness hid her embarrassment.

"All right, then. Good night." He let out a shrill whistle, and in seconds Sam, his horse, was standing beside them. Ben mounted the animal and settled himself in the saddle before giving her a little nod and disappearing into the dark. The sound of hooves on the blacktop road echoed through the night.

When she could no longer hear them, Layla turned and headed toward the house. It was time to put this day to an end. Her days as an attorney were always full but never this emotionally exhausting.

She shook her head, as though anyone were there to see. No, that wasn't entirely true. Defending child molesters and rapists was extremely mentally draining and emotionally exhausting.

The phone was ringing when she stepped through the front door. Too tired to

talk, she almost walked right on by and into the bathroom for a long hot shower, but she happened to catch the caller ID as she passed the phone. The landline was left over from her father. She decided to leave it, since she'd quickly discovered that cell service could be spotty in the mountains. The familiar number stopped her in her tracks.

"Casey!" She gripped the phone with excitement. "Are you stateside?"

"Just got in this afternoon. How you doin', baby sister?"

She groaned. Casey was her brother Rob's best friend. At least he had been until Rob's convoy hit an IED on the road in Iraq. Rob and the three others in his transport didn't make it. Casey was the closest thing she had to a brother now. She loved the way he called her "baby sister," the way Rob had. She only pretended to be annoyed by it. "I'm so glad to hear your voice. You're home, safe and sound."

"Safe, yes. Sound, not so much."

"What's that supposed to mean?" Casey Haines had spent the last eighteen months deployed overseas. She had no idea where. As a Navy SEAL, he often disappeared off her general radar for months at a time.

"I didn't want to worry you."

"Worry me about what?"

"Now don't be getting upset. I'm fine now. Or at least I will be once I get the hang of this thing."

"What thing?" Her heart rate kicked up a couple notches and her knees went weak. Layla dropped into a chair in the hall as a feeling of dread washed over her. "Casey? What happened? Are you okay?"

She could hear him take deep breaths through the phone line. "I'm okay, Layla. Really."

Casey *never* called her Layla. Something was wrong. Very, very wrong. "Casey?"

"It's all right, baby sister. Really. A couple months ago, the transport I was on got shot down behind enemy lines. I've been in a hospital in Germany. Until last week. Now I'm here at Walter Reed for a bit."

"Walter Reed? Shot down? A couple months ago? You didn't *tell* me?" The words tumbled off her tongue in an ambush of emotions. "Your letters… you sounded like you were fine."

"I promise you, I *am* fine. I'm alive. The docs fixed me up real good, and I'm learning how to use this prosthetic of mine. Once I master it, they're gonna let me walk right out of here."

"Prosthetic?"

"I had to bail, Layla. When the bird starting going down, I jumped. My leg was hurt pretty bad. They had to take it off below the knee. But it's okay. I'm alive." He sounded happy and optimistic. She couldn't understand how or why.

Tears rolled down her face, recreating the emotions when she'd received the news about Rob. Casey had called her then too, risking the wrath of his command but not wanting strangers to tell her that her only family member was gone. "You lost your leg, Casey. How is that okay?"

"Because I am alive to tell the tale."

"How long will you be in the hospital? I'll come there."

"No. It's not necessary. You've got a ranch to run, and those animals will get hungry if you aren't there to feed them. I'll be out of here in no time. Then I'll come your way for a visit. I promise."

"Does your mom know you're stateside?"

"Yes. I called her just before I called you. She's already in the car driving here."

"No wonder you don't want me there."

"I'm just trying to spare you the wrath of Hurricane Mary." Casey laughed, and she couldn't help but join him. Mary Haines would have that place turned upside down by morning if Casey wasn't getting the care she thought he needed.

She sighed. "I don't want to get in Mary's way, for sure. Why don't you come out to the ranch for a visit when they spring you from the joint? I could use the company."

"You sound sad, Layla."

"It's just been a really long day. The horse got spooked and threw me. My barn is a mess, and my entire body aches." Too late, she realized she was going on about stupid trivial things when Casey just lost his leg in a war. She sucked in a breath and held back a sob. "I'm sorry. I don't mean to complain."

He chuckled softly. "It's okay to talk to me about things that bother you. The world hasn't changed because I have a metal foot. I want to know you're okay, but I also want to know when you aren't. I promised Robby I would always look out for you."

"Someday you'll have a family of your own to worry about. You have to let go of that promise at some point."

"I won't marry the woman if she expects me to ditch my little sister. Listen, I've gotta run. The nurse is here to get me settled. I'm hoping for a sponge bath if I play my cards right."

"You're such a *guy*, Casey! Seriously though, I'm glad you're okay and alive. I just wish you'd called me sooner."

Casey laughed. "You take care of yourself. Keep your doors locked and a gun handy."

Funny he should say that. "I'm okay, Case, I promise. I'm so glad you called me. I missed you."

"I missed you too. I'll see you soon."

She set the phone in its cradle on the hall table but didn't move from the chair she sat on. Her head fell back against the wall, and she exhaled slowly. Rob had died nearly four years ago. Just two years after her mother lost her fight with breast cancer. Casey was all she had left in this world that even resembled family. If she had lost him too….

"But you didn't. He's alive and well and will be here to visit before you know it." Her words echoed through the empty house.

The four-bedroom, three-bath ranch home was meant for a family. Not one lonely thirty-one-year-old like her. She often found herself wondering why her father had built such a large home if he'd been alone most of his life.

Not that it mattered why he did. She owned it now, and it was up to her to make the best of her new life.

She was an accomplished criminal defense attorney with a long history of wins—who ran from the city with her tail tucked between her legs after winning the biggest case of her career. There had been no glory with that win. Her arguments had set a murderer free and broken the hearts of an entire family.

After her newly freed client had been gunned down on the courthouse steps beside her, Layla questioned everything about her life and all the decisions she'd ever made. Winning that case was no win. It would haunt her forever and served as the number one reason living alone on a mountainside ranch had become her penance.

Hard work and solitude might someday work all the demons from her soul.

Maybe.

Sighing, she pushed her aching body up from the chair and made her way to the bathroom. A hot shower was a must before she did anything else. Like eat a sandwich alone and crawl into a big empty bed. Also alone.

———

"Come on, Sam, let's get you all tucked in for the night." Ben dropped from the

saddle and started loosening the straps. Images of the afternoon replayed in his

mind like an old movie reel. The feel of Layla against his chest when they were on the horse, the length of her sprawled over him on the barn floor. His blood heated and his heart picked up its pace just at the memory of the touch of her lips.

"Get a grip, man." It had been a good long time

since a woman had been in his arms and that had not gone unnoticed by his lonely body.

Sam snorted as Ben ushered him into his stall. "I know, Sam. Women are nothing but trouble." Sam nodded his agreement as Ben shoved a pitchfork full of hay into the stall with the animal.

By the time he finished all his evening chores, his growling stomach let him know dinner was way past due. Farming wasn't his favorite way to make a living, but it was honest work and good for the soul. Everything he had, he worked for, and there was a good amount of pride in that. He liked to think his dad would have been proud of him for making a life of it if he were still alive.

Besides, if he couldn't jump from planes anymore, at least he could get on the back of a horse and have a little of the same feeling of freedom. He missed his old life, more than he would even admit to himself, but this new, solitary one was tolerable. He also missed his family, but they all looked at him with pity. Sure, they tried to hide it, but with all five of his brothers in law enforcement, he couldn't help feeling like he was under constant scrutiny when they were all together.

Now there was his new neighbor to deal with.

Layla Evans disrupted the simple balance he'd constructed for himself.

Ben closed and latched the barn door and headed to the main house. When he bought the place at auction, the roof had nearly caved in and the stoop sagged. Fortunately for him, he'd saved well and could work a saw. The sprawling ranch now looked almost as good as new with the green aluminum roofing and the wraparound porch he added on. Inside had been a total gut job—one Ben was extremely proud of. Especially the master suite, his own private refuge. The king-size four-poster bed hewn from solid cherry sat in the center of the stone floor. A fireplace dominated the wall opposite, and large windows overlooked the small lake behind the house. The bathroom was fit for the most luxurious spa on the planet. The oversized walk-in shower, lined in mosaic tiles, had dual rainfall showerheads and several strategically placed jets that were merciful on an aching body after a tough day in the fields. His muscles were screaming for that shower even as he stripped down to his boxer briefs.

The only item he'd left out were the mirrors. Not a single reflective surface could be found anywhere except the guest bathroom, and that was exactly the way he liked it.

Turning the water as hot as he could stand it, Ben stepped under the spray and let the jets wash over him. Grabbing the soap, he closed his eyes, as was his ritual, and lathered the bar into a mass of bubbles. With a cloth, he worked the lather over his skin, trying hard not to touch the raised lines that crisscrossed his torso.

Twenty minutes later, Ben was sprawled on the sofa drinking a beer and eating a roast beef sandwich. The time for grilling a steak had passed long ago, but there was no way his growling gut would allow him to sleep without feeding it a little something. The eleven o'clock news came on as he downed the last swallow of his drink. The alcohol mixed with exhaustion had a nice warm buzz going inside his brain. It almost blocked out the taste of Layla on his lips. Almost.

THE POUNDING IN HIS HEAD PULLED BEN FROM THE depths of sleep. Groaning, he rolled over and landed with a thud, sprawled on the brown area rug next to the sofa. "Ouch!"

The pounding got louder as Ben rolled on his back and covered his eyes with a forearm, but he couldn't shut out the banging. He groaned. "I really need to stop falling asleep on the couch."

"Ben! Ben! Are you in there?" The banging he thought had been in his head now reverberated through the house, followed by the frantic calls of a familiar voice.

"Layla!" Giving no thought to the fact that he wore only a pair of athletic shorts, he sprinted toward the door and yanked it open. "Layla! What's wrong?"

"I'm sorry. I didn't know where else to go." She was frantic, her hair a mass of wild curls. Feet shoved in rain boots, she wore a pair of blue flannel pajamas with little clouds floating all over them. Even in her obvious distress, she looked adorable. His gut clenched at the thought of what he would find were he to venture under all those fluffy little clouds.

His gut. *Holy hell! I'm not wearing a shirt.*

Turning and running toward the bedroom, he called over his shoulder, "Hold on, Layla! I'll be right back. Come inside."

Maybe she hadn't noticed.

The door closed. He hoped she'd come inside instead of taking off after his abrupt departure. Pulling the first tee shirt he could from a drawer, he tugged it over his head as he ran back to the front door. It pissed him off that he was so flustered. He was used to being calm and in charge.

Layla leaned against the wood door, sniffing. Her eyes were red rimmed and puffy, and her face looked flushed.

"What's wrong?" he asked, trying to calm his breathing as well as his racing pulse. Man, she had such a crazy effect on him.

"It's Chloe. And Zoe."

"Who are Chloe and Zoe?" *Does she have children?* Impossible. They were together all day yesterday and she never once mentioned daughters.

"My cows."

She was crying over cows? "What's wrong with them?"

"I didn't know where else to go. I'm sorry I woke you." Her fair skin flushed a deep red as she turned toward the door. "I guess it's not such an emergency. I'll go home and call the police. I should have done that in the first place."

Ben put a hand on her shoulder to stop her, but the electricity arcing up his arm from the simple contact stopped him in his tracks. He dropped his hand to his side. "Wait. Tell me what happened."

"Is it possible to graffiti living things?" she asked.

"Graffiti a living thing? I don't think so."

"Well, someone graffitied my animals. We didn't notice last night because it was dark, but when I went out to feed them this morning, I saw it." When she stopped talking, Layla took a deep breath.

Ben pictured the animals covered in gang tags, and it almost made him laugh. The last thing he probably should have done. "Let me get some warm clothes on and I'll be right there."

She shook her head. "No. It's okay, really. I'm going to head back. I left without feeding any of the animals. I really am sorry I woke you up. After last night, I just didn't think—"

"It's okay, really. It was past time for me to get up anyway. The couch and I were coming to terms with that when you knocked."

Layla laughed as she walked out the door. "You're a nice man, Ben."

She thought he was a nice man.

Great. He'd been relegated to the nice guy corner. Along with good friend and best buddy. He closed the door and leaned against the smooth wood. He probably should have offered to drive her home. Layla had come to him because he was *nice.* The word made him growl as he headed back to his bedroom.

After brushing his teeth, Ben pulled on a pair of jeans, socks, and a sweatshirt left over from his military days. Slipping into his favorite work boots, he grabbed the keys to his truck and headed to the next ranch up the road.

Being the nice guy that Layla thought he was, he parked in the driveway next to a black Ford Explorer. At least she had the right kind of vehicle for ranch life. The only thing that could have been better was a pickup truck like he drove.

There was no sign of Layla or the two cows. They had to be in the pasture behind the barn. Passing through the stately structure, much nicer than the ramshackle bundle of tinder he called a barn, Ben saw an open door on the far wall. The breezes carried Layla's soft conversation in from the field, and he followed it like a starving man to a hot meal. Every cell in his body reacted to the sound of her voice.

Man, he was in trouble.

Stepping through the door, he caught sight of Layla and her two animals and doubled over with laughter.

CHAPTER FIVE

Layla looked up when Ben stepped out of the barn. Her heart did a funny little skippy thing in her chest as she caught sight of his hair, which was just a little too long, and two-day beard growth.

Her mind rewound to thirty minutes prior when he'd answered the door shirtless with sleep still clouding his eyes. The hard, rippled muscles of a body used to honest hard work, the crisscross of scars that told her he'd been someone's hero, and the strength emanating from him had her thinking things she hadn't considered in a really long time.

As soon as she got back home from her little emotional trip to Ben's that morning, she'd thrown on some work clothes and headed out to the field to take care of Chloe and Zoe. She needed the distraction. Now, Ben stood there in the bright morning sunshine, an incredulous look on his face and she couldn't help but laugh at where life had taken her in the last twenty-four hours.

He started walking toward her, his eyes darting from her to the two cows and

back to her again. "What. Happened. To. Your. Cows?"

"I told you. Graffiti."

Ben shook his head as he walked around first Chloe and then Zoe. "I don't even know what to say to this."

Someone had taken white spray paint and created zebra stripes over Zoe's black hide. Chloe had matching yellow ones across her brown body. Neither animal seemed harmed in any other way as they stood grazing on the new grasses.

"I know." Layla chuckled. "It's not as life altering as it seemed when I stumbled out here half asleep this morning. I've had a little coffee now." She motioned to a travel mug in the grass. "Again, I'm really sorry I woke you."

Ben ran his hand lightly over Zoe's flank. "You still need to report this to the police. It's vandalism and animal abuse."

"I suppose." She had no interested in dealing with anything having to do with the law and police.

"Do you have a problem with the law?" Ben stepped in close, lifting her chin with his finger so she had to meet his penetrating stare. "Are you on the run? In witness protection?" He looked deadly serious but she saw the twinkle dancing lightly in his blue eyes.

"You figured me out. I had no idea I was so transparent," she joked back. It felt good to be relaxed with another human being for a change.

Ben's regular intensity returned. "Seriously, why would anyone be out here messing with you?"

She shrugged. "I have no idea. I was wondering if someone had a grudge against my… the previous owner." She still couldn't think of him as her father. As far as she was concerned, he donated a few sperm, and for that she was grateful, but there was no love lost there.

"Did he have many enemies?"

"Your guess is as good as mine. I honestly didn't even know the man was alive until I received that letter from his attorney."

"What were you before you had all this?" Ben motioned with an arm to the property surrounding them.

"An attorney."

He cocked his head to the side and studied her intently. "You don't strike me as an ambulance chaser."

"Not all attorneys are like those fakes you see on television." She picked up a

sponge from a bucket of soapy water and started to wipe down Chloe.

"I wouldn't do that until after the police and animal control see it." He reached for the sponge but got her wrist instead.

Layla sucked in a breath and looked up at Ben. His eyes were warm as his long fingers slid down the back of her hand and turned it so her palm, and the sponge faced up. "You really do need to make a report, especially after what happened last night."

She nodded. Pulling her phone from her pocket with her free hand, she hit the buttons for 9-1-1, never even trying to pull her other hand from Ben's grasp. While she waited for the operator to answer Ben gently extricated the sponge from her grip—she'd been squeezing it without realizing—and dropped it to the ground.

"9-1-1, what's your emergency?"

"Uh… um…." It was so hard to think over the sparks Ben's touch created.

"Ma'am? Are you okay?" the nasally voice asked.

"What? Oh, yeah. I'm fine." She was captivated by the depth of the shadows in Ben's eyes. So many layers of emotion that she suspected went way beyond what was happening between them.

"Hello? Ma'am? Is someone trying to harm you?"

"Oh, crap, no. I'm so sorry. I've called to report a crime. I need police and animal control."

"What is the nature of your emergency?"

"Someone spray-painted my two cows to look like a tiger and a zebra."

"Someone did what?"

"They graffitied my cows!"

The operator broke down in a fit of laughter. "Are you serious?"

"Why are you laughing? My animals have been vandalized. I don't find that very funny." Actually, she kinda did now, but she hated when people didn't take her seriously.

Ben smiled, obviously amused by the conversation as well.

"I'm sorry, ma'am. I'll send someone out to your place as soon as they can get

there. Next time though, please save 9-1-1 for emergencies. You can call the station directly at their nonemergency number."

"This is an emergency!" she cried into the phone but dissolved into laughter herself when she caught sight of Ben's expression.

"Yes, ma'am, just sit tight. The police are on their way." The operator disconnected the call, her irritation obvious.

"I don't think she liked me very much." Still laughing so hard, tears had begun to roll down her cheeks, Layla tried to return the phone to her pocket but missed and dropped it, right in mud she'd made by squeezing the sponge.

Ben bent over to pick up her phone. He wiped the dirt off it on the leg of his jeans and handed it back to her. "Well, you did call 9-1-1 for spray-painted cows."

"You told me to call the police!" Layla stopped and turned to face him, hands on her hips. "I did what *you* told me to!"

"I said the police, not the emergency call line."

The man was absolutely infuriating. "For crying out loud! Mountain people are so confusing!"

Ben tilted his head to the side, an amused smile teasing his lips. "Mountain people? As opposed to what?"

"Beach people!" Layla kicked at the ground. "Back

in Virginia Beach, you called for help and it came. No one questioned you."

"And exactly how many times did you have to call the emergency line for spray-painted animals when you lived there?" He crossed his arms over his chest, obviously trying to be serious, but she saw that twinkle in his blue eyes again.

"Beach people don't go around tagging people's animals." She motioned to the cows. "You mountain people got the market on that one."

Ben chuckled. "And here you are, a bona fide mountain person yourself."

She gave him her best evil glare, but he just chuckled again. Layla swatted at him, losing her footing on the wet ground. Ben reached out to steady her, wrapping his arms around her and holding her until she caught her balance once more.

Woop! Woop!

"The police are here." His voice had dropped a couple notches to a range that caused little tingles to dance up and down her spine.

"Yeah." She exhaled slowly, in an attempt to steady herself.

"Hello?" a voice called out.

"Back here," Ben replied, still holding her gaze.

She doubted the stranger looking for them had heard.

"Not another damn fake call. I should have known it was a joke. Who in their right mind would spray-paint a barnyard animal?" A uniformed officer appeared around the corner of the barn.

They stepped apart quickly, Layla almost slipping again.

He eyed Layla and Ben, his lips spreading into an easy smile. "Did I interrupt something?"

"No, sir." Ben stepped forward. "Sorry for not hearing you pull in. The lady here and I were settling a bit of a dispute."

The officer shook his head. "Sure looked like the kind of *dispute* I'd like to settle."

Ben gave him a look that she imagined made many lesser men shrink in fear. The cop stood his ground though, staring right back at him until Ben broke the tension by motioning to her. "This is Layla Evans. She's been the victim of some vandalism."

"Vandalism?"

"Uh, Yes." She finally regained some of her composure and could make words again. "Someone trashed my barn last night and spray-painted my cows."

"Your barn looks fine to me." He stepped over and

looked in the doorway, obviously convinced he was wasting his time.

"We cleaned it up last night. I didn't find the cows until this morning. They were out to pasture."

"Well, let's have a look-see." The officer turned toward the field and let out a low whistle. "I'll be a monkey's uncle. Your cow looks like a zebra."

"I know!" The entire length of her career, Layla had dealt with police officers. Most of them were pretty decent guys, but every now and then there was one who tried her last bit of patience—this guy was that one. "I want to make a report."

"Oh, this will make a doozy of a write-up. I can't wait to tell the other guys in lineup. Let me snap a few pictures and I'll be back to take your statement." He ambled across the pasture, whistling a tune.

Layla watched from where she was. Spending any more time than she had to with that officer would not bode well for her should she require his assistance in the future.

"The man is an idiot," Ben said beside her.

"You like that word."

"What?"

"Last night you called me an idiot too. Twice."

He gave her sheepish grin. "I guess I did. Sorry about that."

"You said that too." Layla looked up at Ben. His crystal blue eyes caught the morning sun and reflected off the dark blue of his sweatshirt. The words "Air Force" covered his chest in faded white letters. "Were you in the Air Force?"

Ben nodded. "In another lifetime."

"Well, that ought to do it." The police officer ambled back toward them, grinning. "What time did you say you discovered them?"

"About six thirty this morning."

"When was the last time you saw them looking normal?"

"Yesterday, just before lunch."

He made a note on a little pad he'd pulled from his shirt pocket. "All righty, then. That's about it." He stowed the notebook and pen back where they'd come from.

"That's it?" Layla asked. "You aren't going to ask if I have any enemies or if I have any idea who could have done this?"

"Do you?" the officer asked, raising an eyebrow.

She frowned. "I don't know anyone around here."

"Lady, this ain't an episode of *Law and Order*." The cop bent over, plucked a long blade of grass, and started chewing on it.

"And it's not an episode of *The Andy Griffith Show*

either." Layla held up a hand. "Wait, maybe it's the *Twilight Zone* and I will wake up from a horrible, back woods dream."

The cop rested his hand on his weapon, holstered in his belt. "Do we need to take a trip to the station?"

"You *are* an idiot." Ben practically growled. "We called you for help and you think the whole thing is just a joke."

The cop turned on him. "I've got room for two in the back."

Layla placed a hand on Ben's arm in an effort to calm him some. "No, sir." Ben held his hands up in surrender. "I apologize. It's been a long couple of days and I am concerned with Layla's safety."

The other man relaxed, letting his gun hand leave the top of his weapon. "I'm sorry this is how you've been welcomed to the community but I assure you, it's not the norm."

"Thank you for coming all the way out here, offi-cer," Layla said.

"Not a problem. I'll be in touch if I hear anything."

With that, he turned on his heel and walked away.

———

Layla frowned at the retreating officer. "He *was* an idiot, you know."

Ben laughed, something he'd been doing a lot the last twenty-four hours. "I was right. You definitely have an issue with the law."

"No, just that guy." She shrugged and headed into the barn. "I have to get out and finish checking my fence. I got a little sidetracked yesterday. You know, falling off my horse and all."

"I'll go with you." The words left his mouth before he had time to think about them. He didn't want to spend all day with her again. Did he?

"You don't need to. I'm good. Just don't spook my horse again and I'll be fine." She pulled some equipment off hooks on the wall and started readying the same horse from the day before. "Domino here is good company."

"I don't mind. Let me just run home and get Sam. I'll meet you." *Why can't I stop talking?*

Layla glanced over at him. "Really, it's not necessary."

She didn't need his help. He should just say goodbye and get back to his solitary life of working his own land. He didn't need to get all wrapped up in someone else's business.

Actually, he kinda already had, so what would one horseback ride hurt?

Maybe it would lead to more kisses.

But he absolutely did not want to kiss Layla again.

Liar. Of course he did. The issue wasn't kissing her. It was where kissing could lead. They barely knew each other. To begin with, he had no idea if he could even trust her. Risking his heart again wasn't something he ever planned on doing again.

"Ben?" Layla was looking at him, concern in her hazel eyes. "You all right?"

"Fine." She didn't need to know about the internal battle he was waging. He'd just tell her he had things to do and leave. At least, that was what his brain wanted to say. His mouth didn't listen. "I'm heading out to get Sam. I'll meet you at the creek."

The disconnect between his mind, and… well, every other part of his body grew wider and deeper every time he opened his mouth.

Layla fastened the last couple buckles on her saddle. "I'll be fine. You don't have to meet me."

"I'll see you there in an hour. Wait for me."

Before she could say another word, he strode out of the barn and headed to his truck.

I think maybe I'm the one that's an idiot.

He felt like a lovesick teenager making all sorts of a fool out of himself. Like answering the door shirtless. And driving to her farm after she told him never mind. Or packing a picnic lunch and meeting her at the creek.

Picnic lunch? Yeah, that little development was news to him.

Ben turned on the radio in his truck. An old rock ballad from his high school days filtered out of the speakers. He flipped through the channels until he found something upbeat that had absolutely nothing to do with love.

How had a woman he'd just met tipped the scales of his perfectly balanced routine so quickly?

They were just taking a ride, checking fences. That was it. Being the gentleman his mama had raised him to be. If he could remember that, and keep his distance, everything would be just fine. Once he was confident that the fences were fine, he would go back to his old life. He was just being a good neighbor, the way neighbors were supposed to be.

Ranchers helped each other out. It was an unwritten code. He owned a ranch, Layla owned a ranch, and neither of them knew anyone else, so it just made sense that they work together.

He nodded, as if anyone else were there to agree with him. From now on they would just work together as ranchers. Ben Marshall was perfectly capable of being friends with a woman, no matter what Lauren had said about him being unreachable.

He parked his truck and headed inside. Grabbing the old picnic basket he'd brought home a few months ago filled with his mom's cooking, he ran around the kitchen making sandwiches and packing a lunch fit for an entire baseball team. They definitely wouldn't starve that afternoon.

Because that was what neighbors did. They helped each other and maybe shared a meal while they worked.

Twenty minutes later, after changing into his favorite flannel shirt and some fresh jeans, Ben led Sam out of his stall and saddled him. At exactly one hour from the time he bid Layla goodbye, he pulled up to the creek about a hundred feet from where he'd encountered her the day before. Layla was visible through the trees and brush. His heart did a little dance step in his chest, and his mood instantly lifted at the sight of her. A tiny part of his brain had expected her not to be there when he arrived. Once again, he ignored his brain and let the rest of him lead the way to where she was.

CHAPTER SIX

LAYLA BREATHED IN THE COOL MOUNTAIN AIR AS Domino drank from the stream. Tiny fish flitted around in the clear water, the sun catching their scales every so often to create tiny rainbows. Surrounded by the sounds of the birds and the breeze rustling tree leaves, she almost felt at home.

Some days she really missed the beach. The smell of salt water and suntan oil were like heaven to her, but the fresh, clean country air of her new home made her body feel alive in a different way.

Of course, it could have been Ben Marshall, her handsome, moody neighbor, who made her skin tingle and her heart race as she spotted him through the trees.

She let out a sharp whistle to get his attention.

"You coming, old man? We're burning daylight, you know!"

Her favorite online video guy used that term all the time, and it always made her smile, like it did just then.

Ben crashed through the brush, pulling his horse to a stop just short of where she and Domino stood. He frowned. "Who you calling old?"

It felt good to flirt a little. Since leaving Virginia Beach, she hadn't had any male company. Or any other kind of company, for that matter. Her last big case had damaged her faith and trust in people beyond repair. It truly surprised her that she'd gone to Ben for help earlier that morning. Even more so that she now sat atop Domino, preparing to spend the better part of her day with someone she barely knew. Alone, in the woods, where no one would ever find her body should he turn out to be a serial killer.

"I figured as much of a grumpy hermit as you are, you had to be much older than me." She gave him her best innocent smile, complete with batting eyelashes and a little head tilt.

He raised an eyebrow. "Oh really? Maybe I'm just a young grumpy hermit."

Layla shrugged. "So we agree, then. You're a grumpy hermit."

"If I'm the old one here, see if you can keep up, little girl." Ben nudged Sam and the two of them took off, following the line of the fence that surrounded her property.

Little girl? I'll show him.

Domino saw Sam and followed, running at full tilt while Layla clung to the reins. In a few seconds, she'd caught up with Ben, and then they raced neck and neck for several minutes before Ben suddenly pulled to a stop. Layla and Domino ran right past him.

"Whoa, Dom! *Whoa*!" Domino pulled to a stop so quickly she nearly went flying like the day before, but this time she held on and turned her horse back to where Ben sat waiting. "What's wrong?"

"There's a break in your fence."

"Oh, right. The fence." *Oops.* The wind on her face and the ground disappearing beneath them as they raced through the fields had completely cleared her mind. Being with Ben was so easy, she completely forgot they were on an actual work mission.

He dropped down off his horse and walked over to help her down. Back in Virginia Beach, his chivalry would have annoyed her, but out there in the fields under the sun with horses and a fence to mend, it felt exactly right.

Together they made the repair, laughing and joking comfortably as they worked, less like this was a new friendship forming and more like they'd known each other forever. Layla almost forgot about the ransacked barn and the painted cows and even the reason she left the city in the first place.

"There, that should hold it." Ben sat back on his heels and tossed a pair of pliers over to the tool bag Layla had brought along.

She sat down and leaned back on the soft grass. Folding her arms behind her head, she looked up at the sky. A year ago, she was standing in the criminal court before one of the city's toughest judges defending a filthy child rapist and murderer. How she used to sleep at night she had no idea.

She didn't. That was why she left it all behind.

"What brought you to this corner of the world, Layla?" Ben had stretched out on the grass beside her and was studying the fluffy cirrus clouds intently.

Is he reading my mind?

"You know I inherited this place."

"Why not just sell it and stay in the city like you said you wanted to that day at the attorney's office?"

"Once I got back home and had some time to think, I reconsidered. I guess I just needed a change of pace. Law is an exhausting job."

"So, you were running away too." He said it so softly she wasn't even sure she heard him. The words were a statement, not a question, and made her heart a little heavy. Ben obviously had a few secrets of his own.

"What brought you to the country, Ben?"

"Retirement."

"You're awfully young to be retired."

"From the military. I did a couple tours overseas and it was enough. I wanted something peaceful."

"Well, you don't get much more peace than living alone on a ranch near the mountains." The irony that she and Ben ended up where they were for similar reasons wasn't lost on her. It also struck her as funny that they both had the primary goal of being alone and yet here they were now, together while talking about being alone.

"Yeah, it's been nice. The winters are awfully long though."

"Well, this winter you'll have a little company if you need it. I'm just down the road." She wanted to kick herself as soon as the words left her mouth. Nothing like assuming Ben wanted anything to do with her in the long run. This was just a quick day to get her fence squared away, not the beginnings of a relationship. Her face heated, and it had nothing to do with the sun hitting it.

"That will be nice," Ben replied, his voice still soft. "Very nice."

It did sound nice. A whole lot nicer than facing the family of little Cecilia Owens every day. Okay, maybe not every day, but Derek Owens made sure she never forgot the face of his little girl. Moving away had, in part, been to escape the constant letters, emails, and phone messages she received at work and sometimes at home.

Her boss insisted that she'd done her job and to let it go.

Some job. Helping a child rapist and killer get off the hook.

She lay back on the grass. "Do you prefer ranch life to the military?"

"I don't really have much choice in the matter. Military isn't an option anymore." He sounded a little sad and maybe even a bit angry. Layla wanted to ask him why the military wasn't an option, but it didn't feel like the right time.

They stayed there, side by side, for a good long while, silently watching the clouds amble across the blue sky. Finally, Layla jumped up and held a hand out to Ben. "Come on, cowboy. We've got work to do. If we're gonna be ranchers, then we be better get to doing some ranching stuff."

Ben laughed. "Yes, ma'am." He jumped to his feet and climbed up on Sam. Layla did the same with her own horse and they took off again.

An hour later, they were repairing their third break when Layla's stomach let out a loud growl.

She laughed, embarrassed. And, a little bit disappointed to be cutting her time with Ben short. "I guess I'm a little hungry. I suppose I'll have to head back soon."

Ben reached for the basket he'd dropped in a saddlebag. "You're in luck. I packed us a little picnic lunch."

"I can't believe I didn't think to grab something." Another loud growl sounded deep in her gut.

"No worries. I brought plenty for both of us." He grabbed a blanket from the other saddlebag and spread it on the ground. "Have a seat."

Layla settled on the scratchy wool and watched as Ben, who had seated himself next to her, pulled sandwiches, little bags of chips, and bottled water from an insulated bag. When he handed her a bottle, their fingers touched, and Layla jumped a little at the electricity that once again arced between them when they touched. Ben's eyes locked with hers, leaving her powerless to break the pull between them. His blue eyes, usually so clear and bright, had darkened with a mixture of emotion and… something else. Sadness, or maybe those secrets she knew he had.

After a long moment, he looked away and grabbed one of the sandwiches. He handed it to her. "I hope you like roast beef."

"Absolutely. Thank you so much." She unwrapped the food and took a bite. "Mmmm… so good. Thanks."

"I'm glad you like it. I'm a pro with lunchmeat and anything I can throw on the grill." Ben laughed. "I eat a lot of meat on the grill."

"Nothing wrong with that." Layla opened a bag of chips and popped one in her mouth.

"I went from my mom cooking all my meals to the Air Force feeding me to my… girlfriend." He grimaced. "Although she doesn't really count. She was a terrible cook."

"You have a girlfriend?" A little twinge of betrayal flared at his admission.

Ben shook his head, his expression quickly turning guarded. "Had. We broke up a long time ago."

"Oh." They ate in an uncomfortable silence for

several minutes until she couldn't take it anymore and spoke. "What did you do in the Air Force?"

"Pararescue."

"I've never heard of that. What did you do?"

He leaned back on his elbows and studied the tree branches and sky above them. "I jumped from planes, mostly behind enemy lines and places that were tough to get to any other way, to pull out injured soldiers."

"Wow. I can't even imagine what that was like." His past made hers look like a day at the park. "You're probably the bravest person I've ever met."

Ben shrugged. "It's in my genes, I guess. My father was a cop, and all five of my brothers are in law enforcement. I wanted more adventure and to see someplace other than Virginia, so I joined up right out of high school." He paused and inhaled slowly. "Always be careful what you wish for, Layla."

The pain and sadness in those last few words cut straight through her. She could relate to that in ways even she would never fully understand.

Shifting closer to Ben, she picked up his hand and twined their fingers together. Something about him made her feel safe and a little bit brave herself. Leaning her head on his shoulder, she spoke softly.

"You have no idea how much I agree with you on that."

He rested his cheek against her hair. "I don't know how it happened or why, but I feel more comfortable with you than I have with any single human being in a very long time."

She let go of his hand and shifted so she could wrap him in a hug. "I understand that too, far more than you'll ever know."

Layla let her fingers roam lightly over the soft flannel of his shirt, occasionally passing over one of the raised scars she'd seen that morning. Wanting to ask him about those but afraid to, she traced the outline of one with her fingertip. His body stiffened as his fingers wrapped around her wrist to stop the movement.

"Layla, don't."

"What's wrong?" she asked, looking up at him.

"It's not you. I promise." Those blue eyes of his had turned stormy. Like he had something he really wanted to tell her but didn't quite trust her enough yet to do so.

She pulled away, putting a good bit of distance between them. "Ah, the old 'it's not you, it's me' speech. Don't bother, I'm a smart woman. I can take a hint. Or, maybe I'm not as smart as I think, letting my guard down so quickly with a near stranger."

"No." He reached out and clasped her hand as she started to stand up. "It's not what you think."

She looked deep into his eyes, trying to make sense of the murky depths of blue that stared back at her. "Of course it's not. It never is."

———

How could he possibly make Layla understand? It did sound like he wanted to blow her off when in fact, it was probably the last thing he wanted. In the last twenty-four hours, he'd laughed more and felt happier than he had in years. Being with Layla made him feel like the old Ben. The one without the broken spirit. He didn't want to lose that, and the second she learned the truth about him, how shattered he was, she'd be on her way. He didn't want that. Not yet.

"Look, I promise you didn't do anything wrong. I... I just haven't... been with a woman in a very long time. As a friend or... otherwise. I like you, Layla, but as you've pointed out more than once, I'm a grumpy old hermit. I'm a mess on the inside. You don't want to go there, believe me."

She frowned. "You don't know anything about me or what I want. For your information, I've got a lot of broken pieces too."

"I know enough to know I could really like you. I'm just…." He paused, struggling for the right words, remembering Lauren's final crushing declaration. He was a hot mess, and letting this thing with Layla go any further put her heart in jeopardy—a risk he just couldn't stand to take with her.

"There are reasons I left the military, Layla," he continued. "Reasons that mess with a guy's head. It's not a good idea for us to be friends. It's not that I don't want to be. I'm just trying to protect you."

"We all have baggage, Ben. Do you know what I used to do for a living? I used to *defend* the bad guys. I charged exorbitant amounts of money to convince juries of my peers that these terrible people were innocent of crimes I *knew* they had committed. Why? For money. I liked the finer things in life. Fast cars, expensive wines, fancy trips. I sold my soul to the devil for a paycheck. So don't sit there acting all righteous when you tell me you're protecting me from your demons when mine are so much larger. I guarantee you that."

Ben had no idea how to respond. She wouldn't have understood if he'd tried anyway.

Layla took a long sip of water. He watched her, trying to imagine such a sweet woman working for killers and rapists.

She rose from the blanket. "Thank you for your help today. For everything. I really appreciate it. I can handle the rest now, so I won't take up any more of your time. Go home, Ben. This—whatever it's been—is done."

She turned and walked away.

The conflict was tearing him apart. If he let Layla leave now, he knew she would be out of his life for good. A week ago that's all he wanted. He'd moved to the middle of nowhere to be alone. To wallow in his own self-pity and not have to worry about anyone else getting caught up in the tsunami of his craziness. Now, though? It felt like a newly discovered piece of himself was about to disappear.

She mounted her horse and urged the animal forward. Just before trotting out of view, she stopped the animal, turned and looked at him. "It's been nice knowing you, Ben." And then she was gone.

Too late, he called after her. Either Layla was too far out of earshot, or she'd just ignored him.

"I'm such a fool, Sam." The horse snickered in agreement as Ben tossed the rest of the food and water bottles back into his bag. "Why can't I just tell her the truth?"

Sam whinnied, and he could have sworn the horse had just laughed at him.

Lauren had told him over and over again that there was no hope for him. He was tormented on an emotional level and damaged on a physical one.

He rubbed his hand across his abdomen. Even through two shirts, he could feel every single scar. Layla had done the same thing just a few minutes ago and hadn't seemed to mind. She didn't understand, though. Each one held a memory of pain and torture attached to it. When he slept at night, he relived every last minute of the time he spent as a prisoner of war. How could he put someone else through that with him?

Lauren left when she couldn't take it anymore. That night had been different than the others. He'd woken up on top of Lauren, his hands around her neck. In his dream, she was the bastard who had cut him. She'd told him she hated what he'd become. The anger and fear mixed with pity in her eyes as she threw his grandmother's diamond at him had been burned into his memory forever. When she slammed the door behind her that night, Ben had slammed the door closed on his heart, never wanting to put anyone else through what he had done to the woman he loved more than anything in the world.

Lauren had been frightened. He understood that. Hell, it had scared him half to death. But there had been something more to it. Like she'd been waiting for an excuse to leave and he'd given her the best possible reason. That night, Ben resigned himself to a life alone, where he couldn't hurt anyone but himself.

Something caught his eye in the grass. He walked over and bent down to pick up Layla's tool bag. She'd been so pissed at him she'd forgotten to grab it. "She's gonna need this, Sam. We need to return it."

Sam stomped a hoofed foot and grunted.

"It's not a bad idea, buddy. We'll just drop it off and be on our way. Back to our quiet, lonely life."

Sam shook his head and gave him a "whatever" look. That horse acted too human some days. It was creepy.

He mounted Sam, careful not to drop the tool bag, and took off in the direction of Layla's place, the same mix of conviction and anticipation he felt every time he was about to see her. Determined to do what was best for everyone, he pushed his emotions aside. Until her fields and barn came into view. And he saw her there standing by her two ridiculous-looking cows. His heart did a little jig in his chest as tension immediately built in his muscles. In a dozen lifetimes, he couldn't deny the strong physical pull she elicited from him, so it was up to his brain to take over and hold his ground.

Sam kicked into a gallop and headed straight toward Layla, like he couldn't wait to see her too. She looked up, scowling as they approached. "What are you doing here, Ben?"

"You forgot your tool bag. I didn't know if you would need it or if you had any other tools. Sam and I decided to drop it by, and then we'll be on our way."

She reached up and accepted the bag from his outstretched hand. He noticed she went out of her way to avoid touching him. Served him right. It was what he wanted, after all.

"I'm really sorry, Layla." Why did he feel the need to keep apologizing? He should just turn Sam around and ride off into the sunset. "I've really enjoyed the last couple days, but I don't want you to end up getting hurt." He had to protect his own heart too. It couldn't take any more than it already had.

"Whatever." She shrugged and returned to brushing her cows. "It was nice getting to know you.

We're still neighbors, after all. It's always nice to know who your neighbors really are."

Without thinking, he slid down off his horse and turned her to face him. "I can't leave here until I'm sure you understand that the problem is with me. You've done nothing wrong. In fact, I think you're amazing, and if it were a different time in my life.' He paused to let out a heavy sigh. "Someone told me a long time ago that I'm just too messed up for relationships. Any kind of relationship. The sad truth is she was absolutely right. I enjoy spending time with you, but I can't drag you into my little circle of private torment. You'll end up hating me, and I couldn't live with that."

To his surprise, she smiled and leaned in to press a kiss to his cheek. "Whoever that person was, she was an idiot. You're a good man, and when you're ready to let the world in again, you'll be a much happier person. I wish you a good life, Ben. I just pray you don't let it all pass you by."

She turned and began to shoo Chloe and her calf Zoe toward the barn. Chloe moved slowly, but Zoe took the direction well. Layla never once turned to look back at him. He watched her walk for a minute and then climbed back up on Sam. The horse hung his head. Even he felt sad about leaving.

Ben patted the animal on the neck. "It's for the best, buddy. Let's go home."

Sam whinnied quietly and started a slow walk back toward the trails that led to Ben's property. Even the horse knew what a mistake Ben was making. Layla had begun to have an effect on both of them in just a short time.

The air filled with a deafening *boom.* The ground shook and Sam lurched, throwing his front legs high into the air. Ben gripped the reins with all he was worth, already catching the acrid scent of burning wood. Sam tried to run for the woods, but Ben turned him back toward Layla's barn. Flames shot up toward the sky as smoke quickly filled the air. The horse refused to move, so Ben slid out of the saddle and took off at a run toward the burning structure. Panic started in his gut, spreading quickly through his body, carrying with it a rush of adrenaline that fueled the unnatural speed of his run.

The wind had picked up some as the sun set, swirling burning embers around him as he ran. One settled on his arm, igniting the fabric of his shirt, but he hardly noticed, his mind only focused one thing.

"*Layla!*" He yelled her name over and over, but even he could barely hear himself over the roar of the fire. The heat built, assaulting him in waves. The fabric on his sleeve burned through, the fibers melting into his skin, but still he ran.

Flames engulfed the entire barn, silhouetted against the evening sky. Chloe and Zoe ran across the pasture behind the house, their hooves pounding against the hard ground. Ben stopped short in front of the structure and yelled for Layla once more. There was no sign of her anywhere. Reality hit him like a punch to the gut.

Layla had to be in the barn.

CHAPTER SEVEN

TRAINING AND EXPERIENCE KICKING IN IMMEDIATELY, he pulled his flannel shirt off and wrapped it around his nose and mouth. Doubling over to get below the smoke, he screamed for Layla as he ran to the back door. There was no response.

"Layla!" With burning eyes and his lungs screaming in agony, he charged forward low and fast, stopping near the stalls to call out to her again. "Layla! Are you in here?"

The smoke hung thick and heavy inside, flames licked at the walls, and the roof beams began to creak. The whole building would come crashing down in just a few minutes. Dropping to the ground, he forced his way into the incredible heat, sweat coating him immediately. "Layla!"

A moan sounded just to his right. Feeling around in the dirt and hay, he tried desperately to locate something human. "Layla, if you can hear me, say something so I can find you."

"Here." The single syllable sounded raspy and broken.

He whipped around to his right. "Where are you? Say something else!"

"I'm here, Ben."

Her voice was weak, but enough for him to locate her against the wall just inside the back doors. Flames were working their way along the planks and burned just inches from where she sat. She gasped for air, coughing with every inhale. He pulled her shirt up over her nose and put her hand over it to hold it in place.

"I've got you. Just hang on." Rising to a squat from his crawl, Ben scooped her up. Layla buried her face against the material of his shirt and clung to him. Taking as deep a breath as he could manage in the acrid air, he stood up and sprinted out the back door.

Just as he cleared the building, a loud crash emanated through the air as the entire roof collapsed into the center of the burning structure. Embers rained down all around them as Ben kept running.

"My house. Is my house okay?" Layla murmured.

Sirens sounded in the distance. One of the neighbors must have already called the fire department. He stopped running when he could no longer feel the heat of the blaze and dropped to his knees, still holding her close.

"Layla? Are you all right? Please be okay," he whispered against her hair.

When she didn't respond, he loosened his hold and pulled her from his chest. Her head lolled back and her eyelids fluttered. Lowering his head to listen, he heard only ragged breathing sounds.

"Hang on, Layla. Help is on the way." Stretching her out on the cool grass, Ben pulled his tattered flannel shirt away from his face and made it into a pillow for her before raising her knees into a bent position. Layla had all the signs of shock.

Red lights bathed them as several fire trucks and an ambulance pulled off the road and onto her property.

"Over here!" He jumped up, shouting and waving to the paramedics with both arms as they ran toward him lugging a stretcher and a large, red case full of medical supplies.

Ben gave the paramedics a quick rundown as

they arrived. "No burns that I can see. There was an explosion. She may have been thrown during the blast, so internal injuries are possible. She was barely conscious when I pulled her out, but I think she's in shock now. She needs oxygen. There's going to be smoke inhalation."

"Sir, you're injured." One of the paramedics reached for his arm, but Ben yanked it away.

"I'm fine! Take care of her!"

The second paramedic was already inserting an IV line, but that wasn't enough. Desperation filled him with panic causing him to pace.

"*Sir*," the paramedic said firmly, blocking his path. "Stand still and let me look at that injury. Your arm is badly burned."

Ben glanced at his left arm. There was a gaping hole where the fabric of his long-sleeved tee shirt had melted away, revealing charred tissue. "It's a damn flesh wound. I'm *fine!*"

It was more than a flesh wound. In fact, he'd likely have a nasty-looking scar, but what did he care? It would just be one of many. Layla was the one who needed help.

"Ben's a tough guy," Layla murmured, lifting the oxygen away from her mouth. "If he says he's fine, then he is."

Never had he heard a sound so beautiful as her voice in that moment.

He dropped back down to the grass and grasped her hand. "Layla? What happened?"

"I really don't know. I remember being pissed at you, so I kicked the door open, and there was a loud boom. Next thing I know, my barn is going up in flames and my head really hurt." Her voice was hoarse. A coughing fit racked her thin frame, and Ben longed to hold her close, but the paramedics were strapping her to the stretcher to get her back to the ambulance.

"You can meet us at the hospital," one of the paramedics said with a direct look at Ben's burned arm.

He nodded. "I'll be right behind you."

Layla had her eyes closed and didn't say anything else as they wheeled her away.

The same officer who had responded to the cow call was standing in the driveway next to Layla's truck shaking his head. "What'd she do, man?" the officer asked.

Ben scowled. "What the hell is that supposed to mean?"

"Well, she pissed someone off. This wasn't no accident. No way that barn is gonna burn like that, all sides going at once, unless someone helped it out a bit. That's a big statement to make."

He was right about that. Ben had seen his fair share of incendiary devices in the military. Whoever had rigged the barn knew how to make one heck of an explosive *and* used an accelerant to get a raging fire going. The fact that Layla hadn't been killed instantly was nothing short of a miracle.

"Hey, you want a ride to the hospital? That's a nasty burn you got there." The officer nodded at his arm that was starting to throb as the adrenaline kick wore off.

His first instinct was to say no, but then he remembered that he'd ridden Sam and not driven his truck. Sam was long gone, and it would take too much time to go get his own vehicle.

"Yeah. Okay, thanks. It does hurt a little."

The cop let out a low whistle. "Yeah, I bet it does." He turned to another officer. "Hey, Charlie! I'm taking him to the hospital. You got this?"

Charlie gave him a thumbs-up, so Ben climbed into the patrol car. The pain became a bit more noticeable. Okay, it hurt like hell, but all he could think of was Layla.

This cop better put those damn lights and sirens to good use.

"Thanks for the ride, Officer...," Ben said as the cop slid in behind the wheel.

"Blake. Henry Blake."

"Are you kidding me?" Ben eyed the man, who started laughing as he put the patrol car in gear.

"Yeah, my mom was a huge fan of the television show *M.A.S.H.* Henry was her favorite character. Since our family name is Blake, it worked out well for her."

Ben nodded. "That was a good show."

"The best, according to my mother." Henry turned the truck around and pulled onto the main road.

"Did you see the episode where Henry died in the chopper crash?"

Henry chuckled. "Yup. I avoid riding in helicopters. No reason to tempt fate."

Despite the pain in his arm and his fear for Layla, Ben couldn't help but chuckle. The guy was all right.

"Someone blew up that barn. Someone who really knew what he was doing."

"I know. Didn't I say that already?" Officer Blake flipped on the lights and sirens and took off after the ambulance carrying Layla.

"I mean, he *really* knew what he was doing. Military training, maybe."

The cruiser hit a pothole, and Ben winced. His arm really throbbed. Or the adrenaline was wearing off. Either way, his arm hurt like hell.

At least it's not an angry insurgent with a blowtorch.

The burn had to be third degree. He didn't want to poke at it too much and make things worse but he thought maybe he saw some charred muscle tissue in there upon quick inspection.

They had lost sight of the ambulance. A knot formed in his stomach as the need to get to Layla overwhelmed him.

"Can't you drive any faster?"

"Whoa there, cowboy. I might be a cop, but this ain't no magic carpet. I want to get you there in one piece, you know?"

"Yeah." Ben exhaled heavily, trying to remember the training that had been drilled into his head. Keep the pulse steady and the heart rate regular. He'd be no good to anyone if he freaked out and forgot his mission.

"You're that retired ranger, right? I did a stint in the Army myself."

"Not a ranger. Air Force. Pararescue."

"Still special forces though, right?" Officer Blake turned onto the main road through town. Ben caught a flash of red lights. The ambulance was just up ahead of them.

"Yeah."

"What brought you to the Blue Ridge Mountains?"

"Retirement."

"And being a farmer was your dream way to retire after a valiant military career?" The guy sounded wistful, as though he wished he'd done something more in his military days.

"It was quiet, solitary, and I knew no one would ask questions," he replied.

Instead of taking Ben's hint, Blake laughed. "Son, I ask questions for a living, and I'll tell you what, I've got a few for your girlfriend."

"She's not my girlfriend. We're just neighbors."

"You ran into a burning building to rescue a neighbor?" Blake shot him a sideways glance.

"Wouldn't you?"

"Of course I would," the cop answered without hesitation. "But it's my job."

"And it's what I was trained to do as well. No crash scene is pretty, enemy territory is as hot as that fire, and I would do it all over again."

They pulled up in front of the emergency room entrance. Blake nodded toward the door. "You go on inside. I'm gonna park this bucket of bolts and meet you in there."

The ambulance was just pulling away. Ben jumped from the police car without another word and ran toward the door, suddenly as desperate as he'd ever been to find Layla and make sure she was okay.

The emergency entrance was quiet. Ben ran up to the desk, stuck his head in the window where the admissions person should have been sitting, and yelled, "*Hello!*" His voice echoed through the space, but it took a full thirty seconds for someone to appear as he paced the dingy linoleum floor.

"Yes, sir. How can I help you?" A petite blonde woman wearing hot pink scrubs made her way down the narrow hall from the door she'd stepped out of. "Oh! You're injured."

He frowned. "Don't worry about me. Where's Layla Evans?"

She stepped closer to him, holding a finger to her lips. "Sir, I need you to stop yelling please."

"I need you to tell me where she is," Ben replied, his voice dropping to a tone that was low and deadly.

"Who, sir?" the woman asked sweetly with an easy smile, stepping away from him.

"Fire victim. Just came in on an ambulance."

"Are you family?" She settled down in the chair on the other side of the counter and started tapping things out on a keyboard with nails that were painted the same pink as her outfit.

"She doesn't have any family. I'm a friend."

"I'm sorry, sir, but if you aren't family—"

"It's okay, Sheila, let him back. He's with me." Henry Blake stepped through the doors into the waiting area and flashed the woman a warm smile.

"Officer Blake!" Sheila's cheeks flushed instantly as she lowered her eyes under the intensity of Blake's smile. She was obviously smitten with the man. Ben didn't care if she gave birth to the officer's children as long as she let him see Layla.

"He's harmless, Sheila." Blake winked at her. "You have my word. He's injured too, and could use some medical attention to that burn."

"Most definitely," Sheila gushed. "You can take him on back, Officer Blake. The woman is the only one back there."

"Slow night, huh?" Henry winked and smiled again. "Suppose I shouldn't have said that. Oops."

"Ooh, you said the *s* word!" Sheila fluttered her long nails as she fluffed her straight blonde hair. "I'm blamin' you if things get crazy 'round here tonight."

Fed up with the little sideshow display, Ben started walking toward the door that led to the treatment area. He heard Henry bid Sheila goodbye and follow him.

"Slow down there, hoss. She's fine. Got some good docs working at this hospital."

Ben ignored Henry. Small hospitals made him nervous. Times like this, he missed the military or even being near a big city. Several people wearing scrubs milled around, but no one paid him any attention. Henry got several "Hellos," a couple fist bumps, and plenty of glances from the ladies.

There was only one lady Ben was interested in, and he found her behind the third curtain. She was alone in the small space, a white blanket tucked in around her slim form. An oxygen hose ran to a mask over her nose and mouth, and an IV had been set up in her left hand. She looked peaceful. Ben felt better immediately.

"The nurse says she's asleep." Henry stepped into the curtained room. "I'm going to hang out a bit. I need to ask her a few questions. Hayley here is an excellent nurse. She's going to take care of that burn of yours while I go hunt down some coffee."

"Sir?" A soft voice sounded behind him. "Let me take a look at your arm please."

He turned to face a woman wearing blue scrubs. She couldn't have been more than five feet in height, her red hair tied in a knot and a smattering of freckles covering her cheeks and nose. Nurse Hayley had a pleasant smile and a gentle demeanor. He liked her immediately.

"How's Layla?"

"Poor thing came in here carrying on about someone named Ben. Did she have a loved one that might have been injured in the fire?"

"No, ma'am. I'm Ben. Ben Marshall." Out of habit, he extended his arm to shake her hand.

She accepted his outstretched hand. "Nice to meet you, Mr. Marshall. That is a nasty-looking burn. Let's get you into the next room and clean it up before your lady wakes up again."

He turned back to look at Layla. Nurse Hayley reached out for him, but Ben jerked away before she could touch him. "Mr. Marshall, she's going to be fine." The nurse's voice was quiet and reassuring. "She's just a little shook up. Nothing a little rest and TLC can't cure. Come on, let me fix you so you'll be ready when she wakes."

Ben nodded and let the nurse lead him around the curtain to an adjacent space.

"You just sit right there on the table. We need to get that shirt off you."

Take his shirt off? No way. There was absolutely no way he wanted to explain the hot mess that made up his body to the cute little nurse. "Can't you just cut the sleeve off or something? I don't have anything to wear home."

"Once I clean that wound, I don't want any debris getting in it again. I can get you something to wear home."

He was about to argue, but the look on Nurse Hayley's face told him it was useless to do so. "Can you get me something now? I'll change and then you can fix me up."

Hayley studied him for a long moment. Her scrutiny made him feel transparent as her sharp eyes traced the scar along his jaw and followed it to his neck. Finally, she nodded and left the room. Ben had paced the space twice when the nurse returned and handed him a scrub top.

"Extra-large was the only size we had handy. It should fit your shoulders and give you a little room to move though."

"Thank you," he replied softly.

"Let me help you get that arm out of the sleeve." She grabbed a pair of scissors and cut the material just above the wound, then slid the bottom half off over his hand. "That looks pretty painful."

Ben shrugged. "I've had worse."

Hayley reached up and pulled at the upper portion of the sleeve. "Come on, let's get you out of this thing."

"I've got it." He didn't mean to growl the words. He just didn't want to take his shirt off for her or anyone else.

Nurse Hayley squared her shoulders and looked him in the eyes. "Whatever it is that you don't want me to see, I'm sure I've seen worse. Ten times worse."

"I doubt it."

"Have you seen what it looks like when a man trips and impales himself with a pitch fork? How about what happens when someone slips with a chain saw? Or the damage a piece of rebar can do to human tissue? There is nothing, and I mean *nothing,* that will surprise me or shock me or cause me to gawk. Let's just get you out of this thing without doing further damage to your injury. The sooner I clean you up, the sooner you can get back to your girl in there."

Ben looked at the nurse for a long while, wondering if he could deal with another person seeing the worst of him. There was no doubt the nurse could handle it, but could he?

Hayley reached out with a gentle hand and took the hem of his shirt. "Come on, Ben. It'll be okay. I promise."

He let her pull the wrecked shirt away from his torso and cut the fabric up to the collar. When she finished, she pushed the fabric off his shoulders. He waited for Hayley to exhale or inhale or curse or something, but she didn't.

"There. Now we'll put on the scrub top and get this thing taken care of."

He did as he was told, letting her manipulate the material over his burnt flesh. "Thank you."

"For what?" She looked at him with a smile.

"For understanding. And not asking questions."

"Whatever it was that happened to you, Ben, it's obvious to me that the scars run much deeper than your flesh. Don't let them eat you alive, okay?"

Ben grunted. "It might be a little too late for that."

"It's never too late. Believe me, I know." Hayley set a plastic pan on a silver table in front of him and poured chilled saline solution over the burn. He flinched as the cold liquid cooled the hot tissue. "Sorry, I should have warned you."

He smiled at her. "I've survived much worse."

"I'm absolutely positive you have." She picked up some hemostats and motioned to his arm. "But nothing like this."

CHAPTER EIGHT

BEN BIT DOWN HARD ON HIS LIP AS HAYLEY CLEANED his wound. The chilled saline did nothing to ease the agony of her pulling burnt threads and dead skin out of the burn. The insurgents who'd held him prisoner would have loved this new form of torture.

"Good news is it looks like a second-degree burn. I don't see any bone or much in the way of charred muscle tissue. Of course, the doc is going to have to check it out. Bad news is it's deep enough where it'll probably scar."

Ben shrugged. "Won't be my first scar." The bitterness in his words hung in the air between them.

"Do you want to talk about it?" Hayley asked quietly without looking up from her work.

"Not really. There's nothing to tell. War is rough."

"Were you injured in an attack?"

She poured a little more of the cool liquid on his wound. Ben sucked in a breath, working to hold steady so she could finish her work. "Not exactly."

Hayley pulled a piece of grass from his arm. "What was your job?"

Ben loved his job in the military, and he was proud of all the lives he saved. His time in captivity did nothing to diminish that fact. "I was with a pararescue unit in the Air Force. We were jumpers who went after pilots and their crew who were shot down."

Hayley nodded. "Impressive. You must have some medical training, then?"

"Yes."

"So, you understand how this burn could have been a lot worse. You're a very lucky man."

"You understand how I didn't have a choice, right? Saving people is what I do. It's who I am."

She looked up and smiled at him. "I understand completely. That woman in the next room will be eternally grateful too, I bet. She's special to you." It was a statement, not a question.

"We hardly know each other. I would have done it for anyone." Yes, he would have done it for anyone, but he wouldn't have been in a complete panic, fearing for their life and now sitting twenty feet away from them anxious to get back by their side. As much as he wanted to deny his feelings, Layla had affected him deeply on more than a physical level.

Hayley spread some ointment over the wound and wrapped it securely in gauze. "I don't suppose I have to tell you how to care for this?"

He shook his head. "I know what to do."

She smiled and made a motion to let him know he could get down off the table. "You're free to go, sir."

He jumped down and extended his hand to the nurse. "Thank you."

She accepted his hand but placed her other one on the backside of his. "Tell her how you feel. No one should be alone in this world if they don't have to be."

His only reply was a nod. Nurse Hayley just didn't understand that it wasn't that simple.

As he strode away, she called softly after him, "If she loves you, none of it will matter. You'll be beautiful to her no matter what."

He paused briefly but then kept walking. The nurse meant well, but how could she ever comprehend the memories and images that tormented him every hour of every day?

———

Someone picked up her hand. Layla forced her tired eyes open to see it was Ben standing beside her bed. His expression held a mixture of fear and concern as he looked down at her. Beside him stood the annoying cop who'd responded to her painted livestock. She let her eyes close again.

Ben squeezed her hand lightly. "Layla?"

"Mmmm…."

"Can you wake up a bit? Officer Blake here has a few questions he would like to ask you."

She opened her eyes again, partially. "What do you need to know?" she whispered through dry, parched lips.

The officer held a notebook and a pen. "Did you see or hear anything when you entered the barn prior to the explosion?"

She shook her head slowly. "No."

He made a note on the paper. "Do you have any idea why someone would want to burn your barn down?"

"I don't know. Why would they paint stripes on

my cows?" Her throat burned and her entire body ached. The more she thought about all of it, the angrier it made her. "I don't know anyone here. How could I have enemies?" she croaked.

Ben offered her a plastic cup of cold water, and she accepted it greedily.

"Do you have any enemies from your former life?"

"What do you know about my *former life?*" She sipped the water again.

"Not a thing, miss. Just trying to figure out who has a thing for scaring the crap out of you and destroying your property."

She sighed. "I'm sorry. I don't mean to be diffi-cult, but I just don't know." A thought struck her then. "Well, maybe, actually."

"Maybe?" Blake asked.

"I was a criminal defense attorney before I moved here. I'm sure I made someone mad along the way." There were plenty of people who'd been angry at her throughout her career.

Officer Blake made a few more notes. This infor-mation seemed to interest him. "Ah, I see. Did you tell a lot of folks where you were headed when you left town?"

"Just a few friends. I don't have any local family.

And my old job has my contact information. Just in case."

"Hmmm… do you remember any particular case where you might have, well, pissed the wrong person off?"

A particular case? There were many cases, but only one where an entire family and perhaps the whole city of Virginia Beach would have loved to blow up her barn. "Maybe."

Blake frowned. "Again with the maybe. Could you be more specific?"

She shook her head. "No. Because I don't know anything more specific. From what I've heard, my father was a jerk. He probably made enough enemies for both of us."

"You think he has the enemies? He's deceased."

She shrugged. "Maybe someone doesn't know that."

"I suppose that's possible." Officer Blake made a few marks on his notepad before closing it and putting it in his pocket. "I'm very sorry for the loss of your barn. I hope you had insurance."

"Thank you," Layla replied, the thought of dealing with insurance and cleanup giving her an even worse headache than she already had.

Blake nodded at Ben and headed toward the door. "You need a ride back, Ben?"

He shook his head. "No, thanks, Henry. I'm going to hang out here a bit. Thanks though. I'll find my way later."

"No problem." Henry winked at Ben and smiled at Layla. "I'll be in touch. Hope you're up and at 'em again real quick."

Layla gave a little wave, then waited for the officer to leave before speaking. "Thank you for saving me."

"Oh, Layla, don't ever thank me for that." Ben squeezed her hand gently. "Anyone would have done the same."

She shook her head. "No, not anyone. That place was going up fast. I never would have made it out myself. I just wish I knew who it is who has such a thing for me."

Ben pulled a small vinyl-covered chair over to her bed and settled in it. "Well, you're safe for tonight. I head the doc say he's admitting you."

Layla opened her eyes and frowned. "I don't want to spend the night. I want to go home."

"You took a pretty good tumble. At the very least you could have a concussion. They want to keep an eye on you. Don't you think it's best to just stay put, just in case? It's only for a few hours. It's nearly midnight now."

She sighed, frustrated. "I want to see what's left of my barn and check on the cows and Domino. I don't even know if any of the other horses survived."

"The animals will be fine. The temperatures are good tonight. It's no different for them than one of your cattle out there grazing. When do your ranch hands show up for work?"

"Six o'clock."

"Do you have your cell phone on you?" Ben glanced around the room but didn't see it anywhere.

She nodded and held it up. "It was in my back pocket. I don't know how it survived, but it did. I'll send them a text about the fire and ask them to take care of Chloe, Zoe, Domino, and the other horses when they get there in the morning. I'm so glad they were still outside."

Ben nodded.

As she was texting, the curtain opened and Nurse Hayley stepped into the small room. "It's time to move you to a permanent room for the night."

"Why can't I just go home now?" Layla asked.

Hayley glanced at Ben. "Could you excuse us for a moment? HIPAA and all that."

Ben looked at her. Layla grabbed his hand and shook her head. "It's okay. He can stay."

Hayley smiled. "If you're sure?"

Layla nodded. "I'm sure."

She tapped a few keys on the computer she'd brought with her. "Your bloodwork is mostly okay. Carbon dioxide levels have dropped quite a bit since you came in, so that's good." She glanced over at Layla, nodding at the tube hanging loose on Layla's neck. "That oxygen should still be on your nose. You inhaled a lot of smoke, and the oxygen will help you breathe easier. The doc wants to keep an eye on you for a bit. If things look good in the morning with your oxygen stats and such, you'll be on your way. It's only for a night."

Layla pulled the nosepiece up and breathed deeply of the air flowing through it. It did help. "Okay, fine. But I really need to get out of here in the morning."

"I'm sure you'll be just fine by then." Hayley gave Ben a smile, and he smiled back.

Layla was surprised at the little prick of jealousy she felt watching the personal exchange between them. Either Ben was perceptive or he just had a habit of saying the right thing at the right time, because he turned and took Layla's hand again.

"Nurse Hayley here is a tough cookie. She caused me pain like I've not felt in years cleaning up my burn and did it with a smile."

Hayley chuckled and swatted him lightly with a pair of latex gloves she was about to don. "Big tough military boy was holding back tears."

Is this nurse flirting with Ben?

Layla frowned as she looked from one to the other but had no more time to think about it. An orderly entered the room with a rolling bed and assisted Layla in transferring from the emergency room stretcher to the new bed. As she settled in for the ride upstairs, she turned to Ben. "You don't have to stay here, you know. I'll be fine."

Ben nodded. "I know I don't." He didn't say another word, just followed them to the elevator, Nurse Hayley chatting the entire way. By the time they reached the new room, Layla wanted to smack the other woman.

She didn't understand why the nurse bothered her so much when it had been obvious not so long ago that nothing was ever going to happen between her and Ben. It was for the best anyway. She'd moved to the country to start over and have a little privacy. She didn't need to be worrying about relationships. Especially now that someone seemed to have it out for her.

"Any chance of getting something that might fit me a little better? The guy in the ER didn't have much to offer size wise." The gown she wore barely closed across her chest.

Hayley disappeared and returned with a hospital gown that she handed to Layla. "This is the best I can do for now. Maybe you could call someone to bring you a change to go home in?"

Call someone. That was funny since she had no one to call. Ben was the only someone she'd met since she took over the ranch. She certainly wasn't going to send one of her ranch hands after a fresh pair of panties and a bra. "Thanks. I'll do that."

Hayley left and another nurse came in. "My name's Mary. I'll be your nurse until seven. Is there anything I can get you?" She checked the IV line and oxygen tubes, pushed a couple buttons, and smiled a big come-on smile at Ben. Layla disliked her immediately. Jealousy was turning out to be the soup du jour for her.

"Some ice and ginger ale would be great. My throat is pretty raw."

"Of course it is. You poor thing. I'll be back in a

jiffy." She shot Ben another smile and sashayed her way out of the room.

Didn't she know that no one looked sexy in a pair of scrubs—no matter how tight they were?

"I need to change." Layla swung her feet over the side of the bed. Unfortunately, she moved too fast and got all tangled up in hoses and tubes.

Ben stepped over, catching her. Holding her steady against him, he quickly righted all the paraphernalia.

"You need any help with that?" He nodded at the gown with a wink and half smile.

Ignoring her body's response to his offer, Layla shook her head. "Pretty sure I can handle it. I just need you to step into the hall and stand guard a moment. Or go home if you want. It's late. You must be exhausted."

"I'm fine." Ben strode toward the door and stepped into the hall.

Why was he insisting on staying? She shrugged at the thought. Military folks never left a man behind, right?

CHAPTER NINE

BEN STEPPED INTO THE HALL AND PULLED THE DOOR closed behind him. When he grasped the handle, he caught a glimpse of Layla's bare back as she pulled her shirt over her head. It did things to his insides he'd forgotten could happen.

Layla—the woman who kept trying to send him home. Why was she so anxious to get rid of him? Aside from his whole clumsy "it's not you, it's me" blow-off.

When a good five minutes had passed, Ben rapped on the door. Layla's quiet "Come in" floated through. Her voice was so raspy, it made his own throat ache for her. Where was that nurse with the ginger ale?

As if on cue, Mary stepped in behind him as he

entered Layla's hospital room. "Here's that icy cold drink for you, young lady. You drink up and then get some rest. Doctor's orders."

After handing the drink to Layla, she gave Ben a bright smile and left the room, brushing against him on her way out. Layla caught the intentional move as well and frowned, giving the nurse a dirty look as she walked out the door. Ben held back a smile at the little sign of jealousy. It made him a tiny bit happy that she felt protective. Even if it shouldn't.

Layla sipped through the straw like a man who'd been lost in a desert. Ben pulled a vinyl recliner away from the wall so he could lean back and rest his feet against the bed. As he settled in, Layla eyed him suspiciously.

"Why are you still here, Ben? You made it perfectly clear earlier. I mean, I really do appreciate you rescuing me, more than you'll ever know. I'll be eternally grateful. But your responsibilities are done. You don't have to rescue me anymore. I've got to take care of myself."

She never once looked him in the eye as she spoke, but he noticed the soft pink creeping in over her cheeks and under the oxygen hose. He had really hurt her feelings. Guilt filled him as he remembered their conversation that afternoon.

"I'm sorry I hurt you earlier, Layla. But I was telling the truth. It has nothing to do with you and everything to do with me."

"Why do guys always say that when they're trying to let a woman down easy? It's such a load of crap."

Ben leaned over and turned off the bright hospital room fixtures. The only light in the room filtered in from the partially opened door. He hoped it would be easier to talk in the dark, easier to explain how broken he was and how he wanted to spare her the torment he experienced every day.

"I know it seems that way, but it's not. At least not this time. There's just so much you don't know, so much I can't explain."

"So you've mentioned once or twice."

"Layla."

She held up a hand to stop him. "You don't owe me any explanations, Ben. I just thought… well, I mean, you kissed me. I thought something might be happening between us. I'm out of practice though. Dating has always been second to my career. Apparently I read you wrong. If it weren't for the way kissing you made me feel, I wouldn't even have considered a relationship right now anyway."

There had been no denying the chemistry that existed between them. Even though he shouldn't have kissed her, either time, he had, and his body craved more.

"We don't even know each other, Layla."

She sighed. "I know. That's why I'm so confused. I came to the mountains to be alone. And then there was the barn and my cows. You came along on your giant horse, like a knight in shining armor, and we spent the day together. It all just felt so right. " She paused for so long he thought maybe she'd fallen asleep. But then she spoke, very quietly. "I want you to know I don't go around kissing random guys."

Ben sat forward and took her hand in his own. She was right about the way they felt so right together.

"*I* wanted to kiss *you*. I still do. I want to do more than kiss you. Way more. But under the circumstances, that wouldn't be a very good idea. I'm just trying to protect you, Layla."

"From what?" she demanded.

"From *me*!" he bellowed, forgetting it was the middle of the night in a hospital.

"Everything all right in here?" Nurse Mary poked her head in the room and looked around.

"Fine. Everything is fine," Ben replied, lowering his voice. "Sorry for the loudness."

"You just push that button if you need anything,"

Mary said to Layla, ignoring Ben. She had sure changed her tune.

"Thank you," Layla replied. "I'm sure I'll be fine though."

It pained him to hear the roughness of her voice. A solid reminder that he'd almost lost her. The battle that had waged inside him since meeting her had amped back up to full scale.

When the nurse was gone, Ben tried again to explain himself. "I was engaged once, you know."

"Nope. I had no idea," Layla answered without looking up from her drink. Her apparent indifference hit him right in the heart. "You haven't said much about yourself."

"Her name was Lauren. According to her, I'm not fit for a serious adult relationship."

"Just because it didn't work out with her you consider yourself unable to care about anyone else?"

Man, she isn't making this easy on me. "It goes much deeper than that, Layla. I've seen things, done things."

"We all have regrets, believe me." She sounded sad and a little wistful. Like she had some serious secrets of her own.

"I was in the Air Force. Special forces. My job… well, things happened. Things I could never get over.

Lauren knew it, and now, after messing things up with her so badly, so do I."

Layla set her cup down on the bedside table. "So, because things didn't work out with one relationship, you left your home, your family, and a job I think you loved to come live on a mountain, sentencing yourself to a lifetime of loneliness and self-pity?"

He exhaled slowly. "You don't know what it's like to live in my head. Besides, didn't you basically do the same thing?"

"This isn't about me!"

He leaned forward, looking her in the eyes. "Are you saying you don't have any secrets of your own? Secrets that sent you to the same isolated mountain as me? Secrets that seem to want to see you suffer, maybe even die?"

Layla threw her hands in the air, knocking her cup over. Thankfully it was empty. "I'm not the one saying I want to kiss you but I can't because of my messed up past."

"Maybe not. You certainly haven't shared all the details though, have you?"

"I never kissed you."

"What does that have to do with anything?"

"It has *everything* to do with it." Layla yawned and

pulled her blanket up to her chin. "I think we're done discussing whose life is more messed up. I'm pretty sleepy now anyway."

He jumped up and paced the room, unwilling to accept her dismissal without making her understand. "You just don't get it. I'm broken, Layla, and I'm no good for you. Even if I wish I were with every fiber of my being."

She pounded a fist against the bed beside her. "Don't you think I should get a say in this? I mean, maybe I'm broken too? Maybe we would help each other? You kissed me. Not just once. I *know* you felt what I did. Are you willing to give up what you might have because of what you once lost?"

"I've lost so much more than you know." He sat down again then leaned forward resting his elbows on his knees and holding his head in his hands. "It's better for you if you don't get involved with me, believe me."

"Well, it seems you've made up my mind for me, so there's really nothing else to talk about. Have a good night, Ben. What's left of it anyway." She rolled away from him.

He sat there for a good long while staring at the rise of her shoulders under the sheet and trying to think of something to say that would make things right. Just when he thought he couldn't stand it anymore, he heard quiet snores coming from the bed. Layla had fallen asleep. Out the window, he could see the horizon had begun to turn pink.

The door opened and Hayley poked her head in.

"How's the patient doing?" she asked in a hushed voice.

"She fell asleep finally."

Hayley chuckled quietly. "I meant you. How is your arm? Has it started to throb yet?"

Ben shook his head. "Honestly, I've barely noticed it. I've had much worse."

"I bet. Hey, you need a ride home or something? I heard you came in with Henry Blake. I'm about to go off duty."

He glanced at the sleeping woman and then back to Hayley. He really wanted to go home and put on some fresh clothes, but he didn't want to leave Layla. She would wake up alone, and he didn't like that idea at all. On the other hand, if he ran home, he could change and maybe grab something for Layla to wear when she left the hospital.

"Well?" Hayley asked, her foot tapping the floor tiles. The tiny woman moved like the Energizer Bunny, always in motion. He wondered if she even knew she was doing it.

"Yes. I would like a ride home. It's still early. I can get there, change, and be back here before they serve breakfast." Was he imagining the slight disappointment in Hayley's eyes as she nodded?

"You're a good man, Ben Marshall. She'd be a fool to ever let you go. Come on, let's get you home." She turned and started down the hall.

With a last glance at Layla, he blew her a quiet little kiss, then strode from the room. The idea of clean clothes, maybe a quick shower and a cup of coffee, had become very appealing.

Hayley moved fast for someone barely over five feet tall. He almost had to work to keep up with her as they left the hospital at the employee parking lot. She went to a bright red Jeep Wrangler and unlocked the doors. "Hop in, cowboy."

Ben did as he was told. Hayley left the lot and headed in the direction he indicated. As they drove, she hummed a little bit, and he wondered why she didn't turn on the radio. When they were halfway to his house, he found out why.

Hayley glanced over at him. "So, what's your story, Ben?"

He frowned at the direct question. He didn't want to talk about himself anymore that day. "What do you mean?"

"You're no country boy, and you sure as hell aren't a rancher. I've lived here my whole life, and trust me when I say people talk."

He shrugged. "And?"

"And the things they say aren't pretty."

He shrugged again and turned to look out the window. "I don't care."

"Some people are saying you're an ex-con. Others think you broke out of prison and are in hiding."

Ben burst out laughing. "Seriously?"

"Yeah, seriously. It's that scar on your jaw. It's been said you were in a prison brawl and someone shanked you."

"Good Lord, don't you small town people have anything better to do than stick your noses in other folks' business?" He tried not to sound angry, but in truth, it pissed him off what people were saying. After what he went through, what he sacrificed, so their nosy, gossipy asses could have the freedom to make up such ridiculous lies.

"Hey! It's not 'you people'! I never said I believed them. I think you've got plenty of secrets, just not the juicy kind the people in this town have dreamed up."

"I'm not a felon, I didn't break out of prison, and I never got into a brawl. At least not one I didn't win. I just wanted some peace and anonymity. There, feed that to sharks. I can't wait to hear what they come up with next."

"Ah, it's witness protection, then. I knew it."

He slapped his hand down on his thigh. "I'm *not* in witness protection! My entire family lives less than forty minutes from here. I just like my *privacy*."

Hayley turned the Jeep into the long drive that led to his house. When she stopped the vehicle, she turned to him. "I'm sorry, I didn't mean to upset you. I just thought you would want to know what people have been saying. Especially after the fire last night. People are already talking."

"You think *I* did that?"

She shook her head. "No. I don't. I see the way you feel about that woman. There is no way you would do something to harm her. I just wanted you to know."

"Well, I appreciate you trying to help, but it's not necessary. I'm not running from the law or anyone else." He opened the door and jumped down from the Jeep. "Thanks for the ride."

As soon as the door closed, Hayley hit the gas and spun the tires. Ben watched her until she turned onto the main road before heading to his house. The faster he could clean up and get back to the hospital the happier he would be.

He headed straight to his bedroom, kicking his boots off and shedding his clothes on the way. As he passed the hall bathroom, he caught a glimpse of his reflection in the only mirror he allowed in the house when he pulled off the borrowed scrub top. He put it there for his mother; on the rare occasion she visited, she liked to check her hair and makeup.

Not sure why he did it, Ben stepped into the bathroom and stood in front of the sink. The room was dim in the early morning light, so he could only just make out the shadow of his reflection. In the lightless room, he couldn't see the outlines of the angry scars, although he knew where every single one was by heart.

In a flash of insanity maybe, he reached over and flipped the light switch, bathing his body in a bright glow.

Sucking in his breath, Ben resisted the urge to turn off the light and forced himself to look at his body. With one shaking finger, he traced the longest line, the scar that stretched from just under his left pectoral muscle across his abdomen to just above his right hip bone. The muscles there were taut, as toned as they'd ever been, but the scar remained raised and jagged. Smaller lines, crosses, and burns marked almost every inch of his bronze skin. Had he been fairer skinned like his father, rather than sharing his mother's Mediterranean blood, the marks would have been angry and red. At least he had that to be thankful for.

Lauren had never been able to look at him. Even before she left, the lights always had to be off if they got intimate. She never touched him there either, insisting he wear a shirt. She said it was for him, but he knew better. His disfigured torso was more than she could stand. Hell, it was more than *he* could stand.

Anger and frustration washed over him as he snapped the lights back off.

If Layla had the same reaction to him that Lauren had, it would crush him. But after the night they'd had and the conversation—that horrible conversation where he hadn't even really told her anything— he only wanted Layla in his life even more.

Ben headed to his own bathroom, thoughts consumed by the mysterious woman who'd suddenly dropped into his life. The draw he felt toward Layla far surpassed anything he'd ever felt with Lauren. She was like spring after a cold, hard winter. No matter how hard he tried to tell himself he didn't need her in his life, his heart just didn't want to listen. Nearly losing her in that fire had proven to him just how much he wanted her there.

If he could only come to some kind of arrangement with all the demons in his head. Layla deserved so much more than the man he now was.

The water ran hot in the shower, and the room soon filled with thick steam. Ben dropped his boxer briefs and stepped into the spray. Thoughts of Layla in that steamy room with him filled his mind as he lathered the soap. He imagined the foamy bubbles trailing down her creamy skin, and every muscle in his body tightened. The water washing over her bare shoulders seemed almost real behind his closed lids.

Ben groaned. There was no doubt in his mind that every cell in his body wanted—no, needed—that woman. Was he willing to risk her heart to satisfy his own desires?

He had to keep his distance, for both their sakes. They could be neighbors, maybe even friends, but nothing more—ever. It was for her safety and his sanity.

If Layla rejected him the same way Lauren had, it just might crush his soul permanently.

CHAPTER TEN

THE SUN HURT HER SMOKE-IRRITATED EYES. LAYLA groaned and turned away from the window, getting herself all tangled up in wires and hoses again. The machine beside her bed beeped like crazy.

"Damn it!" she muttered, trying to find the call button for the nurse. Just as she located it, the door opened.

"Everything okay in here?" a pleasant-faced older woman asked as she hustled over to the IV pump and hit a few buttons. The room fell silent instantly.

"Thank you so much," Layla said as she leaned back against her pillows. "Could you close the blinds too, please? That sun is hurting my eyes."

"Sure will." She pulled the curtains closed, leaving only a small opening for natural light to filter in.

"The irritation will go away in a day or two. The doctor will send you home with some drops to soothe them. You are a very lucky girl, you know."

Layla nodded. "So I keep hearing. If Ben hadn't been there—" Her words fell away as she looked at the empty chair beside her bed. He had actually listened to her and left. Her heart ached a little, but she ignored it. It was what she'd wanted, right? "When do I get out of here?"

"As soon as the doc comes by and clears you." The nurse stuck a little meter on her finger and watched as the numbers climbed. When it beeped, she took it away then started removing the oxygen and IV lines. "Your oxygen saturation is much better than last night, almost normal. You're just going to have to take it easy for a day or two. Give those lungs of yours a chance to right themselves." The nurse jotted a few things down on her chart and left.

The room was too quiet. At least when Ben had been there, she had someone to talk to despite the fact that all they seemed to do was argue.

She closed her eyes and thought about what awaited her when she got home. The barn would be nothing but rubble. She needed to call the insurance company and start getting it cleared away. Then there was the issue of shelter for the cows, Domino, and the other horses. She could send her ranch hands to a home improvement store for some kind of temporary shelter. That was about the best she could do for that.

What she really needed to do was find a way home since she'd sent Ben away.

A small part of her had thought he would be stubborn and refuse to leave. Okay, if she were being totally honest, a large part of her had hoped he would see right through her and know she didn't want to be alone. That same part had also hoped he'd gotten over whatever it was that haunted him so he would give whatever it was they'd started a real chance.

A simple touch from Ben set her insides on fire. She wanted to kiss him, repeatedly, every time they were in proximity to each other. Her body longed for his touch, which shocked her. Layla had always been very slow and cautious getting to know people. Her former profession caused plenty of trust issues, so kissing a man she hardly knew was way off base from her usual MO.

Aside from her mom and Rob, who were gone, she'd only ever fully trusted Casey.

Ben, though? She trusted him. Even if she didn't

want to. Something about him told her he'd never hurt her.

Her mind wandered over the memory of Ben's body, stopping at the scar that ran along his jawline. She'd really wanted to ask him about it on several occasions but had refrained. It definitely added to the mystery that was Ben Marshall, and she found that kind of sexy. Mom had always told Rob when he came home with a black eye or a broken bone from a lacrosse game that injuries were attractive to women. She called it the CDI—*Chicks Dig It*—factor. Layla had always laughed, thinking the concept was ridiculous, but now she kind of understood what her mother was getting at. Ben had way more than his share of CDI factor. That nurse last night looked like she wanted to lick him like a cherry lollipop.

That scar though, it definitely had something to do with whatever baggage he carried. The quick glimpse she'd had of his torso combined with his running off when he realized he didn't have a shirt on reinforced that belief. Whoever this Lauren was in his past, she had to be a complete idiot not to realize what an amazing man Ben was, not in spite of the scars but probably because of them.

A light knock at her door sent her heart racing, only to have it skip a couple beats when a nurse walked in with a vase of flowers. "Good morning! Someone left these at the main desk for you." She took a deep breath. "And they smell delightful."

Layla reached for them. "Thank you so much for delivering. I can't imagine who they'd be from."

Hopefully Ben, but she didn't say that out loud.

Once the nurse left, she breathed in the sweet scent of roses before setting the vase on the table beside her. A tiny white envelope fell out of the bouquet and onto her blanket as she moved.

"A card." She popped the envelope open, fully anticipating an apology from Ben. Slipping the little card out, she gasped as she read the words carefully printed on it:

Roses are red.

Violets are blue.

Cats have nine lives.

Apparently so do you.

Watch your back. I'm coming.

She dropped the note like it had bitten her, letting out a little squeal and pressing a hand to her mouth to prevent a scream from escaping.

Someone had intended to kill her in that barn.

The door to her room opened and Ben entered, carrying a backpack on his shoulder. He stopped as soon as he saw her, dropping the bag on the chair. "Layla! What's wrong?"

She motioned to the note lying beside her, not wanting to touch it again.

Ben picked it up. She watched his expression change from curiosity to anger as he read the little poem.

"Where did this come from?" He pointed to the roses. "With these?"

Layla nodded. "The nurse brought them in a few minutes ago. Said they were left at the main desk." A sob caught in her throat. "Oh, Ben! It *is* me. I've been the target all along. Not my father."

He dropped onto the bed beside her and gathered her in his arms. "I'm so sorry. I should have stayed."

"I told you to leave." She buried her face in the side of his neck and breathed in the scent she'd come to recognize as distinctly his.

"I know, but I shouldn't have. I wanted to clean up a little and get you something clean to wear home." He reached for the backpack and handed it to her.

Layla peeked inside to find a long-sleeved tee shirt and a pair of blue sweats, neither of which she recognized. He'd brought her his clothes. New emotions began to replace the fear of a moment before.

"You didn't have to do that." She caught Ben's unique woodsy scent in the bag and inhaled deeply. "But I appreciate it more than you know."

"It's okay. I caught a ride home with one of the nurses, took a quick shower, and brought my truck back with me. I figured you'd need a ride home. Sorry I didn't get back before you woke up." He motioned to the flowers. "Or at least before these showed up. We need to call Officer Blake and let him know."

He smiled at her in a way that was very different from before. It was warmer and more relaxed.

Layla returned his smile. "Thanks for coming back. But I could have called a cab or something."

"You planned on taking a cab dressed like that?"

She looked down at the faded flowered hospital gown. "Maybe the fare would have been free?"

Ben's laughter lit up his face in a way she hadn't seen yet. He actually almost seemed relaxed instead of in the constant escape mode he always seemed to be in.

A knock on the door interrupted their laughter. The doctor, a soft-spoken older gentleman, entered the room and, after doing his assessment, determined her fit to go home.

"I need to change," Layla announced after the doctor left.

"Right. I'm on guard duty. I'll call Henry Blake and report the flowers." Ben turned to leave.

"Wait."

He stopped and looked back at her.

"Is that cop's name really Henry Blake? Like on *M.A.S.H.*?"

Ben laughed. "Yeah. His mom was a big fan of the show. Just leave the card and flowers on the table until I get ahold of him."

She nodded, and he left the room. Layla made quick work of changing into the clothes Ben had brought her. The shirt was just loose enough to hide the fact that she wasn't wearing a bra, and the pants, with the words "Air Force" running down the leg, were a little large even with the drawstring pulled tight, but she didn't mind. At least she didn't have a gaping hospital gown on anymore.

"Okay, I'm done," she called toward the door as she slipped her feet into the shoes she'd been wearing the day before. They were covered with soot but still functional.

Ben pushed the door open, and when he saw her, the breath he sucked in was audible.

"What's wrong?" she asked.

Without answering, Ben closed the distance between them in two long strides. His hand came up and pulled her close by the nape of her neck as his lips crushed against hers. Forgetting the argument they'd had earlier, the flowers and the threatening note, and even her demolished barn, Layla melted against Ben, wrapping her arms tight around him.

———

HE HAD NO IDEA WHAT HAD COME OVER HIM. DESPITE all his best intentions of keeping Layla in the friend zone, the sight of her wearing his clothes had done him in. His body reacted, completely ignoring all the warnings his brain screamed at him. Nothing mattered but the taste of her lips and the feel of her soft curves against him.

His fingers tangled in her already knotted tresses. He caught a whiff of soot and scorched hair, but he didn't care. It just reminded him how close he'd come to losing her permanently when he'd barely found her, and that made Ben hold on more tightly. Her fingers trailed lightly across the material of his shirt. He stiffened as they passed over one of the many hard lines of scar tissue he knew were there, but Layla didn't seem to notice, or care.

"Excuse me. Miss Layla?"

"Oh no," Layla muttered as she buried her face against Ben's chest. He could actually feel the heat of her cheeks through the thin fabric of his shirt.

"She's right here." Ben turned and stepped aside but didn't remove one arm from around her waist.

A young girl with ginger curls and wearing pink scrubs smiled at them knowingly. "I imagine you would like to get out of here as soon as possible?"

Layla nodded, still not looking away from his chest.

Ben chuckled. "Absolutely, she would."

"Well, I just have some papers for you to sign, and then you'll be on your way." She smiled at Ben, a big warm "I know what you're doing today" grin, and then gave her attention to Layla.

Twenty minutes later, they were sitting in Ben's pickup truck and pulling out of the hospital parking lot. He'd asked the nurse for a trash bag after tucking the note back in the rose bouquet. The bag-covered arrangement now sat on the floor of his truck between Layla's feet. Henry would meet them at the police station and take it all in for evidence.

Layla hadn't said much since they'd been interrupted. She was turned to the side, looking out the passenger window. Ben wanted to say something but couldn't find the right words to express what he was feeling. So he just drove.

About a mile from the police station, Layla finally spoke. "Thank you for saving me last night."

"I already told you, there's no need to thank me," Ben replied, surprised that was what she was thinking about when all *he* could think of was getting her back in his arms again.

She sighed. "I know. I just feel like I can never say it enough. Why would someone want to burn my barn down?"

Reality must have been settling in for her. "I don't know. I wish I did."

"This just sucks. I came here to escape evil and twisted people."

"There's evil everywhere, Layla," Ben replied softly, reaching across the console for her hand. "I'm just glad I was there when it happened."

She squeezed his hand lightly. "Me too."

"I'm sorry I've been such an ass."

She looked over at him and laughed a little. "You kind of have been. It's okay, I've been
a little… difficult also."

"There's just so much about me—"

She laughed again. "That I don't know. Yada, yada, yada."

It was Ben's turn to smile. "I'm trying here, okay? Cut me a little slack. I've been on my own for a long time. I'm a little like that guy in the movie when he gets stranded on an island with nothing but a volley-ball to keep him company."

Layla laughed and held her hands up in surren-der. "I guess the two of us are just damaged goods."

"What damaged you, Layla?"

"It's not important right now." She didn't want to tell him. Well, that was definitely something he could understand. He'd barely touched on the surface of his issues, after all.

He let the subject drop since the police station came into view. Officer Blake stood on the sidewalk with a cup of coffee waiting for them.

He waved as they pulled up at the curb, then walked around the truck to where Layla sat.

She opened the door to hand him the vase. "Good morning, Officer Blake."

Henry accepted the flowers in his free hand, careful only to touch where the plastic covered the vase. "Miss Evans! You look a mite bit better than you did last night. How are you feeling?"

"As well as can be expected, I suppose. Thank you for meeting us outside."

Henry leaned in a little to see Ben. "Not a problem at all. How you doin', Ben? How's that arm?"

He motioned to the spot now covered by a bandage and his shirt. "Looks way worse than it is. You know how burns are."

"I'm just glad the two of you survived. That barn is completely gone. It burned hot and fast."

Layla let out a little noise that sounded like a sob. He glanced over at her to see all the color drained from her face. Henry caught the sound too and apologized.

"Sorry, Miss Evans. I don't mean to upset you."

She waved away the apology. "I'm just still working through the loss. I haven't even seen the rubble yet."

"So, what can you tell me about these flowers?"

Layla cleared her throat. "I don't know much. A nurse said they were left at the main desk of the hospital. She brought them to me thinking they were a gift from a friend or family member. There's a little card in there with a threat on it. Ben and I both touched it, just so you know."

Henry nodded. "I'm gonna need the two of you to come in and get printed."

"Right now?" Layla asked. "I just want to go home and take a shower."

Understanding filled his face. "Since it's Saturday and the fingerprint tech is off today, how about I come out to your place in a couple hours to print you? Can you be there too, Ben?"

Layla nodded as Ben replied, "Absolutely. Thanks, Henry."

Henry waved them off as Ben pulled the truck back on the road. Layla stayed silent for most of the ride. Ten minutes later, he turned the truck onto the country road that led to their homes. Five minutes after that, he pulled into Layla's driveway. The air, thick with the smell of charred wood and burned grass, permeated the interior of his truck. The once stately building had become nothing more than a pile of ash. Out in the field, two men carrying buckets moved from animal to animal, probably offering them water.

"It's gone. All of it," Layla whispered.

Ben jumped down from the truck and jogged around to the other side to help her down. She looked so forlorn that he couldn't help but pull her into his arms and carry her across the grassy area toward her house.

She narrowed her eyes at him. "What are you

doing? I can walk."

"Shhh, I know you can. But the doctor said to take it easy for a day or two. I'm just helping you follow doctor's orders." He planted a kiss on her forehead. It surprised him how good—and natural—it felt.

Layla blushed but didn't argue anymore as she leaned against his shoulder. Instead she let out a sleepy little sigh. "I suppose I should follow doctor's orders. I'm too tired to deal with anything now anyway."

"Do you have a house key hidden out here somewhere?" Ben asked as they reached the front porch.

"Under the plant in the corner." Layla motioned toward a large potted plant.

"Is that what you consider hidden?" He set her on her feet and strode to the pot, leaned down, and slid the key out.

She shrugged. "I never expected anyone to look for it but me."

Once they were inside, he locked the door and handed her the key. "I think you should keep this inside for now."

"I suppose you're right. So much for moving to get away from everything." Layla accepted the key, setting it on a table in the hall.

"Why don't you go take a shower? I'm sure it'll help. If you point me in the right direction, I'll whip up some of my famous scrambled eggs. Food is the best medicine."

"Famous, huh? I didn't realize you held such notoriety." She was teasing him. How he'd missed the easy banter he'd had with Lauren before—in the early days of their relationship when he was just a normal guy.

"I have many hidden talents, my dear," Ben teased back, his voice heavy with suggestion.

Her cheeks turned an adorable shade of pink as she caught every bit of meaning. She waved him off as she walked away. "The kitchen is that way. I'm starving, so make a lot."

She disappeared down the hall, leaving Ben pretty ravenous himself. Too bad scrambled eggs wouldn't be enough to curb his appetite.

He headed in the direction Layla had pointed him. Her kitchen was larger than he expected. Warm, cheerful terra-cotta-colored walls displayed pieces of bright Spanish pottery. Dark wood cabinets and stainless steel appliances looked practically brand-new, but it still felt comfortable and welcoming.

He heard the shower turn on as he dug around

for breakfast fixings. Eggs, some fried potatoes, and toast were the perfect pick-me-up after a sleepless night; of course, ten years ago his lack of sleep would have come from an all-nighter partying with friends and not a trip to the hospital, but the company was a hell of a lot better this time around. In the freezer he found a box of frozen sausages.

As he cooked, he tried not to imagine Layla in the shower, a smattering of soap bubbles across her soft skin. By the time he had the potatoes peeled, he really needed a distraction. A small clock radio sat in one corner of the counter. Switching on his favorite country music channel, Ben belted out the words to song after song, trying hard not to let his mind wander back to Layla rinsing off under the shower spray or drying her body with a thick, soft towel—or maybe *him* drying off every inch of her body with that same towel.

By the time the eggs and potatoes were done and the toast had been buttered, he was so turned on that even the melting butter held innuendo for him.

"I didn't know you could sing."

Ben dropped the knife he held. It clattered against the tile floor. Layla stood in the doorway, and—*good Lord*—she was wearing his clothes again.

That and her damp curls forming ringlets around her face about did him in.

He nodded toward her clothes, and she smiled. "They were comfortable. And I like the way they smell."

She likes the way they smell.

It would take sheer luck to get them through the meal if she kept saying things like that.

He put down the spatula he held and turned off the burner the eggs were on. Grabbing a couple plates, he began to dish up the food.

Layla appeared beside him, the scent of hydrangeas wrapping around him. He sucked in a breath, determined to get this meal done and over. She needed to eat, and then she needed to rest. That really was doctor's orders. There was nothing in there about making love on the kitchen floor.

He shook his head, confused by all the thoughts and feelings assaulting him all at once.

Ben handed her a plate, and they sat at the small breakfast table near the window. Too late he realized it was a bad idea. The window looked out over the courtyard and the burned building.

Layla sighed heavily as a single tear escaped the corner of her left eye, nearly breaking his heart.

CHAPTER ELEVEN

BEN REACHED ACROSS THE TABLE AND CLASPED HER hand. Layla looked up at him, a little surprised by the compassion she found in his eyes. "It'll be okay. The insurance company will come out, total it up, and cut you a check. We'll have it rebuilt in no time."

He'd said "we" would have it rebuilt. How had they gone from being constantly annoyed at each other to sitting in her kitchen eating breakfast like nothing bad had ever happened?

"I'm not so worried about that. I just can't stop thinking what would have happened if you weren't here," Layla replied, pulling her hand away to cut her sausage.

A shadow passed over his features. "Truth be told, if I hadn't been such a jackass, you wouldn't even have been in there in the first place. Don't think I don't know that."

"Maybe." She shrugged. "Maybe not. Or maybe the person who set the explosion would have waited. Eventually I would have gone in my barn again. It doesn't matter. You saved my life, and I am forever indebted to you." She said it with a smile, but there was so much sadness in her words.

Ben stood up and looked out the window. "I think there's someone out there." He pointed to the trees.

Layla pushed some food around on her plate without looking up to see where he pointed. "Probably one of the ranch hands surveying the barn."

"I don't think so." He tapped the glass with a fingertip. "There's something shining. Like a light or a reflection."

She looked up then and peered out the window. "I don't see anything."

Ben had already crossed the kitchen and headed to the door. "Lock up behind me, and stay inside no matter what." He glanced back at her. "Please."

Before she could argue, he was out the door and crossing the driveway in long strides. She did as she'd been told and locked the door. The set of his shoulders and the determination in his walk told her to do so and ask questions later.

Ben made it to the trees and pushed his way in through the brush. She lost sight of him for a full minute. Her heart felt as though it would pound straight through her chest as she held her breath and waited. Finally, he emerged from the woods and jogged back to the house. He carried something that she couldn't quite make out.

Opening the door when he reached the porch, Layla stepped aside as Ben came into the house. She locked the door behind him, a simple task she hadn't done much of since she'd lived on the mountain.

"Someone was definitely there." Ben held up a round, black piece of plastic with a sleeve-covered hand.

Layla studied the object. "That looks like a lens cap to a camera."

He nodded. "It is. I thought I saw a reflection or something, and then I found this. Someone was photographing your property."

"Could it have been someone from the insurance company?"

Ben raised an eyebrow at her. "Did you call them yet?"

She stepped back until she could lean on the hall

table for support as realization hit. "No. I haven't had a chance."

"I know." Ben set the cap down on the table. She reached for it, but he stopped her with a hand wrapped around her wrist. "Don't touch that. It may have fingerprints on it. We need to call Henry so he can come get it."

Layla nodded. She knew that—a basic rule of evidence. "Isn't he supposed to come fingerprint us anyway?"

As though it were planned, a loud knock sounded at the front door.

Ben motioned for her to stay put and moved over to the door. She watched as he peered through the peephole, then reached for the doorknob. "It's Henry."

He pulled open the door and let the other man in.

"Good morning, Officer Blake," Layla said.

Henry tipped his hat to her and gave Ben a nod. He carried a plastic box. "I'm sorry to have to do this now, but we really need to get going on your case." He glanced around. "I'd hate to see the arsonist come back."

"No worries." Ben motioned to his earlier find. "We've got something else for you."

Henry eyed the item. "Is that a camera lens cover?"

Layla nodded. "Ben saw someone out by the trees and went after him. He found that when he got out there."

Henry frowned. "What have you gotten yourself into, young lady?"

Layla looked up at the ceiling as though it held all the answers. "I've been trying to figure that out myself."

"Do you have someplace I can set this case?" He held up the box. "I have all my evidence things in here. I need to bag and tag that cap."

Layla motioned toward the kitchen. "Right through there."

She led the way into the kitchen, picking up the two plates left from their meal. Henry set the case on the table and opened it. Pulling on a pair of gloves, he then grabbed a plastic evidence baggie and walked back down the hall.

"Do we go with him?" Layla asked Ben.

He smiled at her and shook his head. "We're good right here." He wrapped an arm around her shoulders. "I'm so sorry all this is happening to you. I can't imagine the stress."

She leaned into his side a little. It felt good to

have someone to lean on for a change. "I just wish I knew why it was happening. It's been months since I moved here."

Henry returned, holding the now full evidence bag. "I'll submit this to be printed also."

"Neither one of us touched it," Ben said. "I used my sleeve to pick it up."

"Good." Henry set it in his case. "Now who wants their prints done first?"

Ben sat at the table. "I'll go first."

Layla watched as Henry pulled out his ink pad and a card and took impressions of each of Ben's prints. When he was done, he handed Ben an alcohol wipe and motioned for Layla to take his place.

She sat down and held out her hands. "You might find me in AFIS."

Henry looked over at her. "Oh?"

She shrugged. "I was an attorney before I moved here. Background checks and all."

"Prosecutor?" Henry asked as he began taking her prints.

Layla shook her head. "No."

"Well, you're much too nice to be an ambulance chaser or a defense attorney." He pressed one of her fingers on the ink pad, then rolled it onto the card.

Layla cleared her throat. "I guess I'm not as nice as you think, then."

Henry stopped what he was doing. "You were an ambulance chaser?"

She shook her head. "I worked for the top criminal defense firm in the mid-Atlantic region."

Henry frowned. "I wouldn't have pegged you for one of those types."

"What's that supposed to mean?" She didn't mean to shout, but the officer had hit an exposed nerve and she didn't like it. Ben stepped in behind her and placed a hand on her shoulder. She knew the move was meant to calm her, but all it did was make her more defensive.

Henry shrugged as he went back to his task. "I just didn't figure you for one to be on that side of the law."

"The way I learned it, everyone is innocent until proven guilty. And the law guarantees every single citizen a chance to defend themselves against their accuser."

Henry handed her an alcohol wipe to clean the ink off her fingers. "You're right, they are. I just didn't see you as the defense attorney type."

"I'm sure Layla was very good at her job," Ben tried to defend her, but he just made her madder.

She huffed. "I was the best. I had everything anyone could want."

"And yet you left it all behind." Henry motioned to the lens cap and then the remains of her barn through the window. "Or maybe not."

Never in her life had Layla wanted to hit a man more than she did in that moment. Her hands fisted at her sides.

Ben wrapped an arm around her from behind and whispered in her ear. "He's a cop. He can arrest you for assault."

She elbowed him in the chest, pulling out of his grip. "I'm not an idiot. I'm not going to hit him."

"But you really want to." Henry chuckled. "Get in line behind my two ex-wives."

Layla walked over to the sink and washed the rest of the ink from her hands. "Why am I not surprised?"

Henry packed up the rest of his stuff and snapped the clasps on the case. "Stay safe out here. Call the station if anything else weird happens."

She stayed in the kitchen while Ben walked the officer out, not caring one bit if it was rude.

It bothered her that he felt that way about her. They barely knew each other. Maybe it bothered her more that he might be a little bit right. She'd only gone with the defense firm rather than any of her other offers based on the salary and benefits. She just wanted to show her mother and stepfather she could make it on her own. It had never been her plan to defend rapists, killers, and other horrible people.

She heard the door close. At least Henry was gone for the moment. She took a deep breath and exhaled slowly, fairly certain Ben would have something to say when he returned.

———

After bidding Henry goodbye, Ben headed back to the kitchen. He wanted to find out why Layla was so defensive about her former job but had no idea how to broach the conversation without alienating her.

He found her at the sink, rinsing dishes.

Walking over to her, he wrapped her in a hug with his body behind hers. She stiffened but didn't pull away, so he took that as a sign to press on. "Do you want to talk about anything? Like maybe why you left the city and a great job to live up here in the middle of nowhere?"

"It wasn't such a great job." She sighed with what seemed like she carried the weight of the world on her shoulders. "I spent my days defending criminals, most of whom were guilty of horrendous things, and the weight of helping so many bad guys get away with what they'd done became more than the money I earned was worth."

"Any case in particular get to you?"

He watched as her expression blanked before a little anger lit her eyes. It was obvious he'd struck a nerve by the progression of emotions that slowly passed through her eyes. He waited to see if she would open up. Finally, she walked over and sat back down in one of the chairs. Ben followed, sitting opposite her.

Layla rested her elbows on the table and leaned her chin on her hands. "I left Virginia Beach because I'm a horrible human being."

"That's not true at all," he replied. "You're kind and caring."

"I was power hungry, money hungry, and every other hungry you can imagine. I took a case that no one else wanted. I defended a rapist and murderer who deserved to fry in the electric chair and got him off on a technicality. Now there's a little girl who didn't get justice and a family that will never, ever be the same. At least her killer will never kill again."

Ben was confused. "I thought you said you got him off on a technicality?"

She sighed. "I did. Someone else shot him on the steps of the courthouse a few days later. It shouldn't have gone down that way though. It's not real justice."

"You were doing your job."

"Tell that to her parents. They didn't buy into the whole fair justice system thing. He should have been found guilty. He *was* guilty."

He reached across the table and took both her hands in his. "Like I said, you were just doing your job."

"Yes. My job." She scowled. "That's why I moved here. I needed to get away from the constant reminders of how awful I am."

She looked so incredibly sad. It pierced straight through his heart. "People keep telling me time heals all wounds."

"I don't believe it. I can't even look myself in the eye in the mirror I'm so ashamed."

Ben knew a little something about that. That morning in the bathroom was the first mirror he'd approached in over two years.

"How long will you hate yourself for this?"

She shrugged. "I guess as long as you hate yourself for whatever baggage you're carrying around."

Well, now, he sure didn't expect that.

"What makes you think something like that?"

"Seriously, Ben? One minute you're kissing me and it's hot as hell. The next you're pushing me away saying it's for my own good or some crap like that. And now we're back to sweet and flirty. I've never known a guy as hot and cold as you, and I've dated some real winners." She pulled her hands away from his and set them in her lap.

This unexpected turn in the conversation caught him off guard. He had no idea how to respond. "Layla—"

She held a hand up to stop him. "It's my own fault, I suppose. I've been lonely. I shouldn't have let you kiss me the first time. Then maybe we wouldn't be here now. In fact, you should probably go home now. I'll get the clothes back to you as soon as I wash them."

"I don't want to leave." He reached for her again, but she avoided his touch.

Layla pushed her chair away from the table and stood up. "You don't owe me anything, Ben. You've gone way above and beyond the neighborly expectations. Thank you for saving me last night. I will be eternally grateful for that." Her voice broke a tiny bit on the last word as she turned and walked toward the sink.

Ben watched a moment as she filled a glass with water and drank it, kicking himself for not saying anything. She was right. One minute he wanted to hold her for the rest of time, the next he told himself he shouldn't be getting involved. He took a few steps toward the door as Layla started washing the breakfast dishes, effectively ignoring his presence.

Any chance he had of finding happiness was about to run down that drain with the food and soap.

Without thinking it through thoroughly, knowing if he did, he'd change his mind, Ben strode toward her. At the same time Layla set her clean glass in the drying rack and turned around, he was there, pulling her against him and crushing his lips over hers. There was a new hunger in him, one that overshadowed the self-loathing and personal torment he'd been nurturing for so long.

"Ben," she breathed against his lips. "I can't do this anymore. You should leave—"

"Shhh," he whispered. "I don't want to leave and I don't think you really want me to either."

He pulled away slightly and studied her. This was

it. Either she would accept him or reject him, but at least he wouldn't hate himself even more for not trying. His body had hungered for Layla from the first moment he set on eyes on her.

"Are you sure this is what you want? I mean…."

"I'm sure." He kissed his way down her neck to the base of her throat. Layla

moaned and he made a mental note, planning to make her do that again and again in the next hour or so. "I told you I'm a real jackass sometimes, but I'm done with that."

Layla wrapped her arms tighter around his neck, pulling him in so close that he lifted her against him and rested her on the kitchen counter. "I have to warn you though, not everything about me is gonna be pretty."

"I don't need pretty. I need you." She ran her fingers up and down his back, over his shirt, but the touch was tentative, as if she was afraid he would jerk away from her again. A part of him wanted to, but he resisted the urge.

He tried not to flinch and cower away when Layla tugged at the hem of his shirt, trying to raise it up. *This is it. Sink or swim time.* He prepared himself for the look of horror and disgust when she saw what had been done to him.

"What's wrong?" she whispered when he stiffened.

"I'm not perfect, Layla," he whispered back against her ear, releasing a heavy sigh.

"Neither am I. Imperfections make us who we are." She pulled back and looked up at him. "Ben? What is it?"

He couldn't speak, so instead he took a deep breath, stepped back, and pulled his shirt over his head, exposing every last scar and deformation in the bright light of the Virginia sun streaming through the windows. Ben braced himself as she reached up with one finger and slowly traced the line that ran from one side of his torso to the other before leaning in and kissing the jagged scar just above his heart.

Layla kissed another one of the marks he'd come to hate over the years and a shiver ran down his spine.

She looked up at him, her expression soft. "Is this what you were so afraid of me seeing?"

He nodded.

She leaned up and kissed him gently on the lips. "These scars are just surface marks. Etchings of where you've been and what you've been through."

"Torture," he managed to get out between dry, parched lips. "I was a POW for several weeks."

"Prisoner of war?" Her eyes grew wide and angry, as understanding set in. "Someone did this to you on purpose?"

"What did you think?"

"I don't know. Not that. How dare anyone do such a thing to another human being!"

By the fierceness of her words and the fire in her eyes, he knew she meant it, and that touched him in a place he'd forgotten even existed. Layla wrapped her arms around his waist and pulled him close, resting her head against his chest right over his heart. He felt the tempo increase and knew she could hear exactly what her closeness was doing to him.

"Why aren't you disgusted?"

She sat back on the counter so fast she hit her head on the cabinet behind her. "Ouch!"

"I'm sorry." Ben rubbed the back of her head, shifting her so he could kiss the injury the way his mother had done to him when he was a child.

She laughed. "I'm fine, really. What do you mean, why aren't I 'disgusted'?"

He took a deep breath and looked into her hazel green eyes. They were dark with emotion but no hatred, no disgust. Maybe not all women were like Lauren. "I told you I was engaged once."

She nodded. "What happened?"

For a moment, he contemplated going into the living room where they could both sit on the couch, but he was sure he would lose his nerve if he let anything sidetrack him, so as Layla sat on the counter and he stood in the kitchen shirtless, Ben told her his story.

"Like I told you earlier, I was in the Air Force. Special forces, part of a group called pararescue. Our job was to go in after pilots and their crew when they were shot down. The last jump I made was behind enemy lines. Only a few of the crew had survived, so we were just trying to get to a rendezvous point for pickup when I was grabbed. Enemy insurgents. They held me captive for ten days before our boys could get in there and pull me out."

"And they did all this to you in that time?" She spread the fingers of both hands over his chest, eyes wide in horror, but not at him.

"They did. There's more, under my jeans, but this is the worst of it."

She traced the line along his jaw. "This too?"

Ben nodded. "It's the only thing I couldn't cover up, so I live with it."

"I like it." She peppered tiny little kisses along the mark. With each one, his blood heated at least ten degrees. "It makes you look rugged and mysterious."

"Wait, Layla. There's more." As much as he didn't want her to stop what she was doing to his body, Ben took her by the shoulders and gently pushed her away. If he didn't keep going, he would never get the rest of the story out, and suddenly he wanted to tell her every little bit. "I spent quite a while in the hospital. It took a long time to stitch everything up and heal the internal injuries."

"What hospital?"

"Walter Reed."

Layla nodded. "I have a brother there now."

"I didn't know you had any family."

"I don't. Casey isn't really my brother, but he's the closest thing I have to family. He was my brother's best friend when Rob was still alive."

"He died?"

"Killed in action a few years ago. He made Casey promise to look after me."

Ben smiled. "He sounds like a good brother. Both of them do, actually."

"They were. Are. Casey's at Reed recovering from losing a leg."

No wonder she got so angry when he told her about the torture. She'd lost someone she loved and nearly lost another at the hands of the same kind of people.

"I wish everyone could be like you." Ben looked down at her and caught his sadness mirrored in her eyes. "My ex-fiancée, Lauren, had all these fancy illusions of being a military wife. She wanted to travel the world, brag about her Special Forces husband. Who knows? She probably got off on the danger I was in all the time. Until I came home covered in cuts and burns and wounds from things I can't even think about without wanting to vomit. I know now she wasn't really in love with me but rather the life she thought I could give her."

"Oh, Ben." She tried to pull him close again, but he stopped her, needing to tell the rest of his story now almost more than he needed air to breathe.

"She took one look at me in the hospital, and I knew something had changed. I thought it was just fear and that it would go away once I was home and on the mend. I couldn't have been more wrong. Things went from bad to worse. She would hardly touch me, and if she did, we had sex in the dark because she couldn't bear the sight of me."

Layla's eyes had filled with tears, but she stayed quiet, perhaps sensing his need to finish his tale.

"The last day we were together, she threw her engagement ring in my face and told me I was too broken to love. I thought she meant I was unable to love her, and I begged her to come back, promising to get help or whatever she wanted me to do. Later, when she was gone, I realized she meant me. *I* was too broken for her to love. She couldn't hack it. All her dreams of the sexy military man going off to save the world, leaving her home to soak up all the attention, had fallen apart when I left the Air Force. I was no good to her anymore. And, as she told me, I was disgusting to look at, so no more sexy man in a uniform."

CHAPTER TWELVE

Layla filled with red-hot anger that grew stronger the longer Ben talked. How could that woman have been so heartless and cruel?

This time she didn't let him stop her. She threw her arms around Ben and kissed with him a passion fueled by her rage at the faceless Lauren for destroying this man's confidence so completely. Her heart ached for the pain he'd been carrying around for so long. No wonder he ran away from his family and his old life.

"For what it's worth, I think the scars make you even sexier," she whispered against his ear as she kissed his cheek. Suddenly she couldn't kiss him enough. Desire to make up for all the love he'd lost since his ex had tossed him aside like yesterday's trash burned hot inside her.

She wrapped her arms around his shoulders and felt the raised lines of more old injuries. She touched them, ran her fingers over them. "I don't know what was wrong with that woman, but I am so incredibly glad she left you."

"You are?" Ben sounded confused and maybe even a little hurt.

"Yes, because now I've found you, and I won't have to share you with her."

He turned back around and gathered her in his arms. She felt hot tears against her cheek. "I'm sorry, Layla. I'm just—"

It was as if every tear he'd held onto for years fell all at once.

She wiped away some of the saltiness with her fingers. "Never apologize to me. Not ever."

He buried his face against her shoulder for so long her shirt was wet when he pulled away and looked at her through watery, red-rimmed eyes. She could see embarrassment darkening his gaze. "I don't know what came over me."

"It's okay to cry, Ben. You're human, and you've been carrying a terrible weight around with you for so long. Your Lauren was an idiot. An idiot and a fool."

"She's not 'my Lauren.' If I never see or talk to her again, it will be too soon."

"I'm really happy to hear you say that. Now, if you would just follow that hall over there to the last door on the left, I would like to show you what a fool she was by kissing every last inch of your body at least twice, maybe more. Maybe a lot more."

Ben's emotional gaze burned through her as he followed her directions to the bedroom. All the way there, Layla alternated between anger and gratitude. Angry that another human being had inflicted such physical pain on Ben and downright pissed off that someone he loved had in essence treated him worse than his torturers. On the other hand, if those things hadn't happened, she wouldn't be in the arms of a man she was pretty sure she might be close to falling in love with.

He placed her carefully on top of the colorful patchwork quilt Layla had found in a closet when she took over the house. After replacing the mattress, box spring, and sheets, the handmade piece made her feel homey and comfortable. It almost seemed sinful to have it present for what she was about to do with Ben, who was stretching out on the bed beside her.

She didn't have a problem with that at all.

Ben adjusted the pillows behind her head. Layla couldn't stop trying to touch him. She was as hungry for the contact between them as a man starved for food, but he stayed just out of reach of her embrace.

"Come here, Ben." She couldn't hide the desire in her voice even if she'd wanted to.

"Shh…." He held a finger to his lips as he ran his hand along the bottom of her

shirt, slipping just inside. The muscles in her abdomen trembled beneath his fingertips. With that hand, he slowly inched her shirt up, exposing her stomach. Layla shivered.

"Are you sure—"

"Oh yes," she replied before he could even finish his question.

Sitting up and pulling her with him, he yanked the tee shirt over her head and then pushed her gently back against the pillows. "It's been a while. I might be a little out of practice." The pink tinge of embarrassment in the russet skin of his face made her smile.

"Just like riding a bike, I promise."

As she contemplated pushing him over and

climbing on top of him, Ben leaned in and took her lips. The kiss was tentative at first, not like his usual passionate "go big or go home" approach. Wrapping her arms around his neck, she pulled him on top of her, opening her lips and granting him the access he hadn't yet asked for. To hell with it. The guy had no idea what he wanted. She would just have to show him.

The feel of his hard chest against her softer one was glorious in all the ways one could imagine. So many nights of sleeping alone, the other side of the bed cold and empty, could be coming to an end. Layla hadn't been alone as long as Ben, but she'd been lonely for a lifetime. She needed this as much as he did, if not more.

Trailing kisses from her lips to the line of her jaw and down her neck, Ben let out a little moan that Layla echoed. His touch sent sparks shooting over every last one of her nerves. Her entire body was electrically charged and ready to spontaneously combust if he didn't do something soon to relieve the agony.

"Ben, please." She reached for the button on his jeans as his mouth moved a little lower on her chest.

He stiffened for a second, and Layla was certain he was about to flee like a startled deer, but he slowly relaxed. He nodded against her chest, and she felt a shudder run through him before he spoke. "Do you want me to close the shutters and pull the drapes?"

"Now why would I want you to do that?" Layla slid her hands up his abdomen until she held his face.

Avoiding her gaze, Ben kept his eyes focused on the place where her heart beat. Just having him stare at her like that, so focused, increased the rise and fall of her chest.

"Look at me, Ben." He did as she asked. "I am not Lauren. I am not repulsed by you. Can't you see that by now? Everything—and I mean everything—about you turns me on. Now, stop holding back on me, would you? I want the lights on and the windows open. If it'll make you believe me, we can go out back in the middle of the pasture and do this."

"I'm sorry." He shook his head vigorously, tossing a lock of thick dark hair onto his forehead. She reached up and pushed it away.

"Don't apologize anymore. There's nothing to be sorry about. I want you, you want me, and it's Lauren's loss."

He seemed to consider what she said for a moment before jumping off the bed. Afraid he was leaving, she started to speak until she realized he was pulling off his boots and dropping his jeans to the floor.

"That's so much better." Layla grinned, feeling giddy. "Now get back over here."

Ben did as he was told, but instead of stretching out over her again, he hooked his fingers in the waist of her borrowed sweatpants and yanked them down. She giggled. "Now I feel like the teenager getting it on for the first time. Did you lock the door?"

He laughed, a relaxed sound that just added to the excitement of the building anticipation. "Nope. Let your folks walk in. I don't care."

"My folks? You're ridiculous!"

As he kissed her again, her heart pulse pounded in her ears.

The pounding got louder. And louder.

Ben sat up. "Did you hear that?"

"What?" She gasped, reaching for him again.

"Someone's knocking on the door."

"They'll go away if we just ignore them." Her voice was hoarse with need as she tried again to reach for Ben at the same time he rose from the bed.

"Wait here." The undertone to his voice unnerved her.

The pounding had grown more insistent. Ben

pulled on his jeans, settling them over his hips but not bothering to button them as he put his shirt back on.

"What's wrong?" she asked, grabbing her shirt and pants and scrambling back into them.

"I don't know. Were you expecting any visitors?"

"I don't know anyone, and I haven't called the insurance company yet."

Grabbing a gun off the bureau she hadn't realized he'd been carrying, he held a finger to his lips. "Stay out of sight and be quiet."

She thought about arguing with him, reminding him that he wasn't her father or her boss, but something in Ben's eyes told her do as he asked.

He made his way down the hall toward the front door. Layla trailed behind, quiet as a mouse despite the fear setting up camp in her insides. What if it was the same person who'd burned her barn down and painted the cows?

Why would a criminal knock on the door?

The thought made sense, but then why was Ben holding a gun, ready to shoot whoever it was that kept pounding on the door?

She watched from the corner of the hallway as he looked through the peephole. Her heart raced, and her body shook just a little. Ben was all business.

Standing behind the door, he grasped the handle and yanked the door open, pointing his gun at the chest of whoever was there.

"Who the hell are you?" Ben demanded.

"Who the hell are *you*?"

She heard a click as Ben readied his weapon. His voice was low and deadly. "I asked you first."

"Whoa, man! Put the gun down!"

It can't be.

She stuck her head around the corner and yelled, "Ben, *no*! It's okay!"

———

"DON'T SHOOT! BEN! *DON'T SHOOT HIM!*" LAYLA RAN around the corner and to the front door, putting herself between him and the man at the door.

"Get out of the way, Layla." Ben motioned gently with his gun.

Ignoring him, she turned and grabbed the guy on the porch up in a hug. "Casey! I'm so happy to see you!"

"What's the deal with GI Joe here, baby girl?"

"He's just protecting me. I thought you were in the hospital?" She took Casey's hand and led him inside, stopping to close and lock the door.

"When you didn't answer any of my calls, I let myself out of Reed and jumped the first plane out here."

"I was in the hospital too. I'm sure you saw my barn." She turned at motioned at him. "If not for Ben, I wouldn't be standing here talking to you." Layla reached over and touched his arm. "Ben, this is Casey Haines. The one I was telling you about before."

"Nice to meet you." He reached out to shake the other man's hand, still eyeing him suspiciously. "Name's Ben Marshall."

"Ben Marshall?" Casey studied him with a curious look. "You military?"

"Yeah."

"What branch?"

"Air Force. You?"

"Navy. Used to be SEAL till the enemy had their way with me." Casey eyed him silently for a minute. "You special forces?"

"Pararescue. Retired a couple years ago."

"It can't be." Casey's brown eyes lit up, and he broke into a huge smile. "Layla, do you know who this man *is*?"

"Do I know you?" Ben didn't recognize the young man, but he'd dealt with so many people under high stress that he rarely remembered faces, just events.

"You're a damn legend, man. You know that, don't you?" Casey clapped him on the shoulder, taking Ben by surprise.

"Do you know him, Case?" Layla looked back and forth between the two men, her confusion evident.

"That's Ben Marshall."

"Well, I know who he is, but how do *you* know him?"

"Oh, I don't personally. But everyone over there knows who he is. He's a damn superhero."

"I wouldn't exactly say that." Ben tried to brush off Casey's obvious admiration. "I just did my job."

"Just did his job. You hear that, Layla?" Casey laughed and grabbed Ben in a big bear hug. "You know who he is?"

She nodded. "Yeah, he's my neighbor. You're acting a little nutty, Casey."

"I'm sorry. It's just not every day you get to meet a real hero. Ben was there when Rob went down."

"My brother Rob?"

"Yeah. He saved half the crew on that one single-handedly."

"Really?" Layla looked at him with admiration. "I heard that was a big mess.

Enemy everywhere."

"It was. The story says Ben held off a group of insurgents while they evac'd Rob and the rest of his guys."

"I was just doing my job," Ben repeated. He hated thinking about that night. He wished this guy would just shut up already. He was about to spill all of Ben's secrets to Layla, things he wasn't ready to share with her yet.

Casey wrapped his arm around Layla's shoulders. "You got any bottled water, baby girl? It was a long flight."

Ben followed them into the kitchen, but only because he didn't want to miss anything Casey said. Not because the jealousy clenching his gut made him.

"So, the night Rob was shot down, Ben here and his crew jumped in after them. I heard there were a dozen enemy insurgents and Ben held them off by himself. Until they snatched him up."

Casey's words hung there in the silence for a full minute. Ben watched Layla's face as understanding slowly crept into her green eyes.

"You were there when my brother died?" she asked quietly.

"I didn't know your brother, but what he says is

true. I mean, I was there."

Casey looked from Ben to Layla and back again. "You didn't tell her, man?"

"We only just met a few days ago," Layla whispered, never taking her eyes off Ben. "We haven't had the opportunity to… talk about everything."

"Yet he met me at the door with a gun pointed at my chest." Casey gave him a look full of questions.

"Layla has had a rough couple days. You saw the burnt pile of rubble out there that used to be her barn?" Ben was more than happy to get the focus off him until he had a chance to be alone with Layla and explain the rest of his secrets to her.

"Yeah, what happened out there?" Casey turned to Layla and took her hand. "When I talked to you earlier in the week, you said everything was great."

"It was. And then it wasn't. I don't know what's going on, but someone is very unhappy with me."

Casey pulled her into a hug and that green monster in his gut punched him hard.

"You know what? I think I'll be heading out. The two of you obviously have some catching up to do, and I don't want to get in the way." He turned to leave the room, ignoring Layla as she called after him. Long strides took him toward the front door, and he was on the porch before she caught up with him.

"Ben, wait."

"It's okay, Layla. I'm a big boy. I understand."

"Understand what?"

He continued down the steps and headed toward his truck. He heard footsteps running behind him but didn't slow his pace. He needed space. And time to think. If only Casey hadn't brought out all his worst memories in a five-minute conversation.

Layla reached him just as he started to climb behind the steering wheel.

"Ben, would you just hold on? Please!"

He looked down into her eyes, and it was damn near impossible to ignore the plea he saw there. "What do you want?"

"Why are you leaving?"

"You've got other things on your mind at the moment. I'm just getting out of the way." He reached for the door to close it, but Layla inserted herself between him and the door.

"There is not and never has been anything between me and Casey. He's family to me."

He shrugged. "It's no big deal, Layla. You don't owe me anything."

"Ben! Will you just listen for a minute and stop

being so damn stubborn!"

He stepped down out of the truck and crossed his arms over his chest as though that would protect him from the heartache he was about to endure.

"I told you Casey was my brother's best friend. They knew each other their whole lives. Casey always looked after me the same way Rob did. You know I didn't know my real father."

Ben scowled. "He's awfully touchy with you, for being like a brother."

"You're jealous."

He didn't answer. There was no reason to. It was a new emotion to him, but she was absolutely correct.

Layla stepped forward and wrapped her arms around his neck, pulling his lips close to hers. "The only man I care about in that way is acting like a damn fool right now."

With a low growl that surprised even him, he spun Layla around, backing her up against his truck, and crushed her lips with his. He felt desperate in a way that was completely foreign to him. Ben had been in a lot of dangerous situations, had been held against his will, tortured, and nearly left for dead, but nothing had ever made him feel as many emotions as he did at that moment. He ran his hands down her arms, the need to touch her so over-whelming it almost made him crazy.

"Hey! You two want to get a room or something?" Casey yelled to them from the front porch.

Layla pulled away just a little and giggled. "I forgot he was here."

"Yeah, me too," Ben whispered against her lips. "Any chance of getting rid of him?"

She swatted his chest. "He just got here!"

"I hear there's a nice motel in town."

"I can't send my brother's best friend to a motel!"

"I meant for us." Ben actually laughed at the look of mock horror on her face.

"Why, Ben Marshall, just what kind of girl do you think I am?"

"One I would very much like to be alone with right now. We have a lot to… talk about."

"Talk, huh?"

He grinned and she giggled. This teasing and flirting felt so foreign to him. He liked it though. A lot.

"Come on, you two!" Casey called. "If you can separate yourselves for a little while, I'll take the two of you out to eat. I'm dying for a thick, greasy cheeseburger. Do you know what kind of food they give you in a hospital?"

CHAPTER THIRTEEN

THE THREE OF THEM SAT AROUND A TABLE IN THE local diner, Layla felt grateful it hadn't been a booth where she had to pick who to sit with. Seeing Casey was one of the highlights of her life since moving to the ranch, but Ben was doing things to her insides just by being close to her. They needed to find some time later to have a long talk about all the things he hadn't told her. When that talk was done, they definitely had other things to attend to.

Ben's knee brushed against hers. Her mind went immediately back to her bedroom earlier in the day, warming her cheeks at the thought of what might— scratch that, *would* have happened if Casey hadn't interrupted them. Suddenly, as happy as she was to see her brother's best friend, she was nearly as anxious for him to leave so she and Ben could pick up where they'd left off.

She snuck a glance at Ben as he made polite conversation about Casey's trip from DC. When he caught her looking at him, he winked. Somehow, she was certain he knew exactly what she was thinking about, and it had nothing to do with delayed flights and changes in weather.

"I still can't believe I'm sitting here in the presence of military royalty." Casey banged a fist lightly against the tabletop. "Damn it, I feel like I should be bowing or something."

Ben's sun-bronzed complexion darkened, and Layla could see the embarrassment in his blue eyes. "Seriously, I was just doing what I was trained to do. What we were both trained to do. You know you'd have done the same."

Casey shook his head. "You have heard the stories being told about you, haven't you?"

Ben shook his head. "Nope."

"Remember, Ben is retired now," Layla said. "It's probably been a while since he talked shop."

Ben gave her a grateful smile before turning back to Casey. "I've been out too long. I don't have a clue what's happening over there anymore, but as far as I can see, you were just as dedicated to the cause as I was, so I would hardly say I'm anything special."

Casey nodded his understanding. "Gotcha, man. No more shop talk. I'm having a tough time being out of the thick of it for so long. How's retirement treating you? I need to get used to the idea myself. No way the United States is gonna let me jump anymore, not with this hardware I'm sporting." He kicked his leg out from under the table and pulled up his pants leg showing off his shiny prosthetic limb.

Ben nodded and smiled. "It's nice. Quiet. I like ranch life."

Layla caught the glance he sent her direction and returned it with a smile.

"How about you, Layla? Things working out okay here? Aside from the obvious mishaps."

"It's different for me too, Casey," Layla said. "A tougher life than living at the beach, but the work is honest, and until a couple days ago, I felt safer than I had in a long time."

"Are you absolutely positive someone burned your barn down?"

Layla nodded. "I think so."

"Arson is suspected, yes," Ben answered.

"Any idea who?" Casey asked.

Layla shook her head. "Not a clue. The only person I know around here is Ben, and he was with me all three times."

"Three times?" Casey shot her a confused look.

"Yeah, the day before it burned, someone ransacked my barn. That night, they also spray-painted my cow and her calf."

Casey choked on the soda he sipped. "Painted your cows?"

She nodded. "Yeah."

"One looks like a zebra and the other a tiger," Ben added.

Casey laughed, slapping his knee with his palm. "Holy crap. You people grow 'em crazy out here."

"We were wondering if my... if the previous owner might have pissed some people off."

"But why go after you? This is a small area. I'm sure everyone knows he's dead."

"They might also know I'm his daughter."

"Right. I forgot about that." Casey took another long swig of his beer as the server placed their meals on the table in front of them. She delivered Casey an extra sweet smile as her breasts brushed against his arm.

"Well, hello there...?" He tugged a lock of her hair that had come loose from her clip.

She giggled. "Stacy. My name is Stacy."

Casey held out his hand to her. "Well, isn't that a coincidence. My name's Casey. We rhyme."

"Stacy and Casey. I like it." She gifted him another smile, this one with something other than sweetness in it. "I don't remember seeing you around before. You in town for a visit?"

"I suppose you could say that. I'm here checking up on my little sister over there and trying to figure out if this is a place I could settle down in." He tapped his prosthetic. "War injury here. Limits my retirement options."

"Oh?" Stacy gushed, flipping long red curls over her shoulder. "You're a soldier?"

"Was. My SEAL days have come to an end."

"A Navy SEAL? How *heroic*!"

Stacy was obviously enamored by Casey, and Layla could see it doing wonders for his ego. As long as she'd known him, her friend had been quite the ladies' man. Losing his leg had probably worried him in more ways than the obvious. Miss Stacy didn't seem to care though, as her eyes openly wandered across Casey's broad muscular chest and solid strength of his shoulders.

"Stacy! Order up!"

She glanced toward the food window and then back to Casey.

"I hope I see you around here again before you leave town." She licked her lips and batted her heavily mascaraed eyelashes.

"Oh, I'm feeling pretty good about that happening." Casey gave her one of his hundred-watt smiles and a wink. "The... menu here is pretty appetizing."

Stacy sashayed her way across the diner as Casey watched her.

"The menu, huh, Casey?" Layla swatted at him with her napkin.

"I'm a starving man, baby girl. Been sharing my quarters with other dudes for way too long."

"Look, man, you can borrow my truck if you want to take the girl out tomorrow. If Layla here doesn't mind." Ben winked at her, and she nodded agreement.

"Absolutely, Casey. Maybe you'll fall in love and stick around so I'll have some family nearby." And give her and Ben a chance to be alone for a bit to finally finish what they had started earlier that day.

Casey glanced toward the table where Stacy was taking an order and nodded

slowly. "Yeah, I might just take you up on that. You sure you wouldn't mind?" he asked Layla. "I mean, I did come all this way to spend time with you."

"It's fine, Casey. You deserve a little fun in your life after all you've been through."

A dark shadow passed over his expression so quickly, Layla wasn't even 100 percent sure she'd seen it. Then he broke into a huge smile. "Well, then, don't mind if I do. You got a pen, little sis?"

Layla dug a pen out of her purse and passed it to Casey. He jotted his cell phone number on a paper napkin and sauntered as best he could with his new leg toward the young waitress. Layla and Ben watched as he whispered something in her ear, making her giggle and flush a pretty shade of pink. He passed her the napkin and whispered something else in her ear. She swatted him with the towel she was wiping a table with.

"He sure knows how to work it with the ladies," Ben commented. "Even with his leg like that, he oozes confidence."

"Yeah, it's a talent. Casey is one smooth operator."

"A guy could get jealous of those talents." He actually looked a bit sad as he watched Casey chat up the cute waitress.

"You have *nothing* to be jealous of, sir. Casey is

like a big brother to me. There has never been anything more to it than that."

"You're much prettier than she is." Ben's compliment caught her off guard. She didn't feel particularly special in a pair of jeans and an emerald green sweater.

"Oh, I don't know about that."

"I do." He was looking at her with so much desire that his blue eyes had gone almost black.

"Okay" was all she could think to say as he stared at her so intently that Layla felt her very soul melt from the heat of it.

He leaned over and whispered in her ear, the same way Casey had with the waitress. It was Layla's turn to flush a deep crimson. She felt the heat in her face spread down her neck, over her chest, and continue down. Reaching over, she squeezed his hand, unable to respond with words to his proposition.

———

FOR THE FIRST TIME IN AS LONG AS HE COULD remember, Ben felt happy. Layla had just turned a lovely shade of red at the suggestions of what he would rather be doing at the moment, and it made him want to do those things even more. She'd seen his scars, heard his story, and still wanted him. A terrible weight had been lifted. He felt so free he thought maybe he could fly.

"I'm guessing Casey will be all right even if he can't go back to the Navy." Layla nodded toward the man as he flirted with their server.

Ben nodded, feeling a little wistful. "I get the feeling that not much could keep your friend down. I envy that for sure."

"You're right about that. Casey's personality is magnetic. People are always drawn to him. I think part of it is he is okay with who he is."

"I don't know how he does it. All I've wanted to do since I got out of the hospital is hide. Casey, he's showing off his disability like it's a medal of honor."

She reached up and pressed her palm to the scar on his face. "It is. He, and you, honorably served your country at great personal cost. You earned those scars protecting your fellow Americans. Seems like something the world ought to know, if you ask me."

His heart filled with so much emotion as her words hit him. He'd never considered himself a hero but Layla was right about one thing—he loved his country and the job he did and he earned his scars.

Taking her hand in his, he pressed a light kiss to the inside of her wrist. "So, how long do you think he'll be here?"

"Ben! You keep saying that, but he just got here!"

Ben laughed. "I know." He leaned in and pressed a kiss to her forehead. "I feel like there's so much I don't know about you. So many things I want to tell you about me, too."

"There is." She smiled and kissed his cheek. "But we have plenty of time to get to know each other."

"Yeah." He tangled his fingers in her hair and pulled her close enough to kiss her forehead.

When Layla pulled back, she held his gaze for a moment before looking away. How much of him could she actually see? The hurt and the pain he'd carried for so long, or the excitement he felt at the prospect of a future with a woman he could very well come to love.

"Hey, Casey! Your burger is getting cold," Layla called over to her friend.

He turned and offered her a half wave. "I'll be right there!" They watched as Casey took Stacy's hand in his and lightly kissed the back of it before returning to their table.

"I was working, you know." Casey grinned as he took a big bite of the burger on his plate.

"You've always had a hand on the table," Layla teased. "It's just a matter of whether you chose to play it or not."

"Unfortunately, things have changed a little for me since the... accident. A lot of the ladies are turned off by titanium accessories."

"Take it from me, buddy, not all ladies are the same." Ben leaned over and planted a kiss on Layla's lips.

Casey cleared his throat. "Come on, you two. It's not time for dessert yet."

Ben pulled back reluctantly. It felt so damned good to kiss a woman again. *This* woman in particular.

"So, Casanova, what are you and your new lady friend doing tomorrow?" Ben finished off his burger and wiped his hands on a napkin. "That was really good."

"I suggested a movie, and she countered with a picnic in the park. I didn't want her to be embarrassed to be with me in public, and she wanted to show me off to everyone in town. I like this little place you've moved to, Layla."

"I'm liking it more and more every day myself. You know, you could invite Stacy out to my place.

There's a stream on the property—perfect place for a picnic."

Casey shook his head. "Might be a bit far for me to walk. I'm still getting used to this contraption of mine."

"There's a road. It's rough but manageable. You can take my SUV."

"Or my truck," Ben said, with a wink. "Better yet, take my four-wheel ATV. Get her to hold on real tight."

Casey shrugged and grinned. "I'll have to check with my date. Damn, I love saying that again. I'm really thinking of staying here."

"I thought you loved living by the ocean," Layla said.

"If I ever see another grain of sand in my lifetime, it might be too soon." Casey let out a long, wistful sigh.

Ben couldn't help himself. He started laughing and couldn't stop. He reached over and clapped Casey on the shoulder. After so many months in the deserts overseas, he had no interest at all in beach vacations either. "I know what you mean, man. I really do."

Laughing and joking. Sharing a meal with other people. These were the things Ben had missed the most during his self-imposed exile. That and simple human contact. All he could think about now was getting that simple human contact on with Layla. Every single soft, creamy inch of her.

"Ben?" Layla said.

"Sorry. I guess I got lost in my thoughts for a minute there. What did I miss?"

"You ready to head out?"

Was he ready? Only if he could take her with him. "Sounds good. Let me get the check."

"Already done, my man," Casey replied with a wink toward Stacy. He rose from the table and headed over to where the waitress stood by a cash register. Ben watched the other man as he paid the tab and admired him for embracing his new abilities so well.

Of course, there was no Lauren in Casey's life slowly stripping away all his self- confidence. Why hadn't he realized what she was doing when he was with her? His whole life might be different.

And you might not have met Layla.

Based on the way his heart rate kicked up when she was near, that in itself was more than enough to have lived through hell with Lauren.

He rose from his seat and offered a hand to Layla. She accepted it and let him tuck her hand in the crook of his elbow as they made their way to the door of the diner. If they gave Casey a few minutes with his new interest, Ben might be able to steal a kiss or two from his own. Now that he'd done it once or twice, he wanted to keep kissing her every chance he had. She must have read his mind, because she led him around the side of the diner to a little spot out of the glow of the streetlights and the restaurant's windows. They were barely out of sight when she had her arms around his neck, pulling his lips to hers.

"Mmmm… I've been wanting to do that since you took that first sip of your soda," Layla said as they separated slightly.

"Me too." He kissed her again.

"I couldn't stop watching your lips as they sucked the straw." She giggled, and Ben pulled her in tighter to his chest.

"You're adorable," he whispered as he nibbled her ear lightly.

"Adorable?" She sounded offended. "How about sexy, hot, or… no, sexy will work."

"How about all of the above and then some?"

She smiled. "Why, Ben Marshall, are you trying to sweet-talk me now?"

He grinned back at her. "Is it working?"

"Depends on what you are trying to get out of it."

He trailed tiny little kisses from her earlobe to the base of her neck. She squirmed against his chest, but that just made him hold her closer. "I think you might know what I want out of it."

The muscles at the base of her neck quivered as he ran his tongue across the little hollow there. "Mmm…."

"I can't leave you two kids alone for a minute." Casey chuckled behind them.

Ben hadn't even noticed him approaching. He was losing his instincts. Or he was just too damned distracted to care.

Reluctantly, he released Layla and stepped back, but he didn't let go of her hand as they walked to the truck. Ben felt like a teenager in love for the first time, and it was freaking awesome.

"So, what's the word, Casey? Your girl coming out to the ranch tomorrow?" Layla asked as they all climbed in to the truck.

"She liked the idea of a private stream to picnic by." His eyes twinkled like a kid on Christmas morning.

"Good! I've got stuff at the house to make a great lunch with. I'll whip something up for you in the morning," Layla said.

"No need, ma'am. I've got a few culinary skills of my own." Casey cracked his knuckles and then flexed to show them his cooking muscles.

"You're a nut, Casey."

"I know, little sister, and thanks to Rob, you have no choice but to put up with me."

The ride back to Layla's place was pleasant. They laughed and joked and discussed classic rock and the horrors of modern television. It felt good to be normal again. Talking to the trees and the squirrels had gotten old a long time ago. He just hadn't realized it.

Now that he'd found Layla, he didn't want her out of his sight. Not that he had any claims on her just yet, but if things went well, one day maybe they would never be apart again.

You're getting way ahead of yourself, buddy.

God, how he hated that little voice of reason in his head. Still, when Layla turned to step down from the truck, he jumped from the driver seat and ran around to meet her. The air still held the scent of charred wood from the barn fire, stars twinkled in the clear sky overhead, and he'd never seen anything more beautiful than Layla.

"Here, Casey, let yourself in." She tossed Casey the keys, which he caught easily with one hand.

"You play a little ball in high school?" Ben asked.

"First base." Casey grinned and saluted Ben before jogging slowly toward the front porch.

"It breaks my heart to see him like that," Layla said quietly. "He was always so lively and active."

"I don't think the damn thing has done all that much to slow him down, actually," Ben replied, thinking about his pathetic ways of dealing with his own injuries. He admired Casey for staying the course and remaining strong. Hell, he just made himself a date and he'd only been out of Walter Reed for like twenty-four hours.

Ben reached out and pulled Layla to him. "There, that's better," he murmured against her lips. "I wish I could take you home with me, maybe finish what we started earlier."

"If Casey—"

"I know. You have to stay with your guest, but he better be in a separate room." It had been ages since he'd teased someone. Being flirty was fun, especially when he could see her cheeks turn that pretty shade of pink he was really starting to enjoy. The full moon lit her from behind, and she looked like an angel. His very own angel—since meeting her had essentially saved his life from the living hell he'd resigned himself to.

Ben pressed a kiss to her lips. He'd intended it to be a sweet goodnight kiss, but just the slight contact lit a fire low in his abdomen that quickly consumed him.

"Ben." She pulled back slightly and looked up at him. "Not that I don't want this—I *really* do—but I need to get inside now."

He leaned his forehead against hers and held her face gently. "I know. It's just…."

"Just what?" Layla prodded.

Ben studied her for a long moment, reading so many emotions in her beautiful eyes but unable to bring himself to say what he really wanted to.

She took his hands in hers and brought them to her lips, placing a gentle kiss on the knuckles of each one. "I'm not going anywhere, Ben."

How did she read him like that? It was unnerving, like his thoughts fed directly into her brain.

"It's just that now that I've found you," he murmured, "I never want to let you go."

CHAPTER FOURTEEN

LAYLA WATCHED AS BEN'S TRUCK PULLED AWAY FROM her drive. His parting words echoed her own feelings. How had she gone through a life without him and thought she was happy?

She shook her head and took a deep breath. The answer was simple: she never knew what she'd actually been missing.

Before he left, they exchanged cell numbers, and Ben had promised to text in the morning so they could plan something for when Casey went on his date. Her feet barely touched the ground as she turned and made her way toward the house.

"Hey there, little sister." Casey waved to her from the sofa. He looked exhausted,

and it worried her.

"You okay?" She sat next to him on the couch and took his hand in hers. "You look a bit tired."

He yawned and stretched. "Been a long day. Between the flight and having your boyfriend threaten to shoot me—"

"He's not my boyfriend!"

Casey laughed. "That's it?"

"What?"

"You're mad that I called him your boyfriend but not a word about how he aimed a gun at me?"

She laughed. "Oh please, Casey. You know he wasn't going to shoot you."

Casey shook his head. "Nope. Pretty sure he would have if I'd tried to hurt you. That dude is in deep for you."

She felt the heat in her cheeks and the smile she couldn't stop spread wide. "You think?"

"Oh, come on. He couldn't take his eyes off you. His hands or lips either. Every time I turned around, he was touching you."

"*Casey!*" She grabbed a throw pillow and whacked him in the chest with it.

He fell back against the sofa laughing. "Hey, I just call it like I see it."

Layla leaned back against the sofa also, sighing.

"He's a really nice guy. It's been a long time since I've met a genuinely good man."

"That's quite a scar on his jaw."

"Yeah."

"You know how he got it?" Casey took the pillow she'd whacked him with and situated it behind his head.

"Yes. Sort of. You already know he was a POW for a while."

"They cut him up good, didn't they?"

Layla let out a long sigh as she remembered the marks she'd seen on Ben's body. "You have no idea. Oh, Casey. It must have been so awful for him."

He stretched out an arm across her shoulders and pulled her close. "Yes, baby girl, it probably was. And he'll carry that with him for a long time. Maybe forever. I know." He nodded toward his leg.

"How does one get over something like that?"

"They don't. They just learn to live with it day by day. I'm still working on that."

She squeezed his hand. "I'm so glad you survived. I couldn't bear to lose you too."

"I'm too ornery to go down without a fight. It's going to take some getting used to, though. Retirement came on me a little earlier than I planned, but I'll figure it out."

"Stacy the waitress seemed happy you're here."

Casey grinned. "She is fine, I gotta say. I'm not sure what will come of it, but it feels good to do something normal for a change. It's been a rough road coming back."

"I can't even imagine. I wish you would have told me. Let me help you through it."

He exhaled. "You had your own life going on."

"Casey, you're always a part of my life. Rob loved you like a brother, and so do I."

"Whatever happened with that big case of yours? The one with the Kiddie Killer?"

She looked away as her eyes filled with hot tears. "I did my job."

"Layla?" He squeezed her shoulder lightly. "What happened?"

"I ran such a good case that the jury couldn't find him guilty. He got off and was set free to rape and kill again."

"Oh, baby girl." He pulled her into his chest. "I'm so sorry."

"For what?" she asked, wiping at the dampness on her cheeks. "That's what I was hired to do. I'm a damn good defense attorney. I should be proud." The words sounded every bit as bitter and empty as she felt. "Someone shot and killed him as we left the courthouse after the verdict. I thought I would be happy about it, but I just wish he'd gone to prison. Then I wouldn't feel so guilty."

Casey pressed a kiss to the top of her hair. "Now I understand the move out here. I wondered why you didn't just sell this place when you found out about it."

"I don't know. I thought about it. Almost did it. Then one day I looked into the eyes of the parents of that little girl and realized I was selling my soul to the devil every time I got one of those creeps off the hook. I'm an evil, awful, horrible person, and because of me, every little girl in the country could have been in danger tonight."

"That's a bit harsh, don't you think? Our justice system guarantees every American the right to counsel and the right to a fair trial with a jury of their peers. Those peers found him not guilty."

Tears ran down her cheeks. "Because I convinced them."

"Come on, Layla, you are not single-handedly responsible for all the evils in the world."

She sat up and dried her eyes on the corner of her sweater. "I know. It was just time for a change."

A loud crash sounded from the front yard. Layla jumped from the sofa and ran to the front door.

"Layla! Wait! Don't open the door!" Casey called after her as he followed. "Do you have a gun?"

She whipped open the front hall closet and grabbed two shotguns. Tossing one to Casey, she yanked open the door, her gun poised and ready.

"I told you—holy crap." He let out a long, low whistle.

"My truck...." Layla scanned the area of the driveway lit by her security lights and saw nothing but her truck—with a huge hole in the middle of the windshield.

Together they made their way to the vehicle. She stopped to look at the gaping hole and the large rock that sat on the front passenger seat.

"Oh, man." Casey called to her from behind the vehicle.

"What?" She walked to where her friend stood. "What the hell?"

In the same paint used to paint her calf like a tiger, the word "Bitch" was scrawled across the tailgate of her truck.

"Is there something you haven't told me?" He sounded worried.

"No. I don't know what's going on!" She threw her hands in the air, nearly tossing her shotgun. "I give up! Whoever you are, you win! What do you want from me?"

"Layla, let's get inside." Casey took her by the hand and started leading her back toward the house. "We need to call the police," he said, louder than necessary.

"Okay," she responded, understanding that he was hoping the person who had vandalized her truck would hear.

When they made it into the house, Casey closed and locked the door behind them. Layla grabbed the phone and dialed the number for the police. This—whatever it was—was getting way out of hand. Her stalker had succeeded in scaring her, and she hated him for it.

Ben found himself whistling as he parked his truck and headed to the barn to feed the horses and other animals. He couldn't remember the last time he'd even turned on the radio let alone whistled a tune. How had so much changed in such a short time?

He felt the weight of his cell phone in his pocket and smiled. Exchanging numbers was such a nonevent, but it made him feel like a teenager with a crush. He couldn't wait to get inside and send Layla a goodnight message. Happiness had been out of reach for so long. He felt a little desperate to hold on to it now. It was surreal how lighthearted he felt. He kept expecting the other shoe to drop—to find out Layla was secretly in love with Casey or something.

Finishing up in the barn, Ben closed and latched the door and headed to the house. He needed a hot shower and a good night's sleep filled with dreams of Layla in his arms. Smiling to himself, he unlocked the door and stepped inside. The house felt empty. Whereas a week ago the emptiness would have offered him solitude, now it represented a lack of Layla.

He almost pulled out his phone and called her to come over, but he resisted. She needed time with her friend to catch up. The guy had lost a leg in a war and acted like it was just another day on the job. Generally good at reading people, Ben had a tough time figuring Casey out. Was he really as okay with the forced retirement and disfigurement as he seemed? If so, he could stand to take a page out of Casey's playbook. Maybe then he wouldn't have wasted the last two years of his life since Lauren left, totally hating himself.

Ben headed to his bedroom and shucked off his clothes. Standing naked, he did something he'd pretty much never done since it happened—he looked down at the crisscross of scars marring his once decent-looking torso. He traced the ugly lines the way Layla had. She hadn't been disgusted by them. His chest and abdomen were still strong and hard, the muscles well defined by the work that accompanied ranch life. The scars suddenly seemed secondary, like a series of tattoos telling a story. One he wished he could forget, but his story nonetheless.

With a finger, he followed the long scar from just above his hip bone to the inside of his thigh. One particularly mean captor had threatened to turn him into a woman that night, dragging a long, sharp blade across his skin frighteningly close to his manhood. Someone had stopped him, a young woman whose face Ben never saw, but he felt her kindness in the way she tended his wounds later that night.

He never understood that. Once every few days, they'd sent in a female to bathe him with a sponge and tend to the worst of his injuries. The only conclusion he'd come to was they enjoyed torturing him and hadn't wanted him to die too quickly of an infection.

It didn't really matter. He was alive and solid, and that was all that mattered now, right?

His shower wasn't a race to get clean and away from his own body like it usually was. He took the time to enjoy the heat of the water, feel the suds washing away not only dirt and sweat but painful memories and self-loathing. When he stepped out of the stall and wrapped a towel around his waist, Ben felt like he'd just washed away a lifetime of anguish and torment. Climbing into the king-size bed, his favorite splurge of his redecorating, he pulled his cell phone off the bedside table and pulled up Layla's number.

Just wanted to say goodnight. Can't wait to see you again tomorrow.

He stared at the words on the screen before hitting Send. Did it sound desperate? Pushy? The indecision made him laugh out loud. He was a trained military man, special forces, used to outwitting the enemy and making split-second decisions, yet he couldn't decide if he should send a text message to a beautiful woman or not.

What the hell did he have to lose? He hit Send and waited.

An hour later, he still held the phone in his hand, frustration and self-doubt returning. But it was well past midnight. Maybe she'd gone to bed early, before he sent the text. She'd had a really rough few days, after all.

Or she's busy giving her friend *Casey a welcome home treat.*

The logical part of his brain knew that wasn't true, but that nagging little voice that had worked so hard at convincing him how useless and unattractive he was to women for so long had started to dance and cheer inside his head again.

Throwing the phone onto his nightstand with a string of his best curses, Ben pulled a pillow over his head and willed a dreamless sleep to come.

———

When the first light of day made its way through the window, Ben had just fallen asleep. No message from Layla ever came, and try as he might to explain it away, he couldn't.

"What the hell is wrong with me?" he asked the ceiling above his bed. "I'm a soldier. Soldiers don't pine over women and text messages."

He jumped from his bed, hit the bathroom, and

then pulled on some jeans and a tee shirt. As he dressed, he thought about Layla and trying to text her again.

What if something happened to her?

Oh God, what if whoever was trying to get to her actually did?

While Ben lay in bed feeling sorry for himself, had Layla been in danger?

He shook his head. No, Casey was there and as highly trained as Ben was. The nature of their relationship was odd to him, but one thing Ben was certain of was that Casey wouldn't let anyone hurt Layla. Still, he felt the overwhelming need to get to her place and check on her.

As he rushed through his morning chores in the barn, he felt his cell phone vibrate in his pocket and unlocked the screen. A message from Layla popped up.

Sorry I missed you last night. Had another visit from my... stalker? Not really sure what to call him.

Ben dropped the rake he was using to move hay and straw and ran to his truck.

Another visit? What the hell happened this time?

Henry Blake's patrol car was parked in front of Layla's house when he got there. Her truck was gone. Fighting back the panic that threatened to overtake him, Ben jumped from the driver seat and ran across the driveway. Taking the steps to the porch two at a time, he yanked open the door without knocking.

"Layla!" he bellowed, his voice echoing through the house. "*Layla!*"

"Ben?" Layla stepped into the hallway. "What are you doing here?"

"Are you okay?"

"I'm fine. Why?" She stepped forward and put a hand on his arm. "You're about to hyperventilate."

"You said you had a visitor last night. I thought… I was worried…."

"I'm sorry. I had no idea it would upset you so much. I should have waited until you came over later to tell you."

"Tell me what?"

"Oh, hey, Marshall. Nice to see you again." Officer Blake stepped out of the kitchen. Ben had a quick flashback of the last time he and Layla were in the kitchen, and his muscles tightened a little in response to the memory of his lips on hers.

"What's going on, Blake? Why are you here?"

"Your lady friend here had another unwanted visitor. Someone vandalized her vehicle."

So, Layla had been dealing with another attack and he'd been pining away about an unanswered text message. He was becoming all soft and fluffy. What happened to the tough airman he'd been trained to be? *Special forces, my ass.*

"You weren't hurt?"

She shook her head. "Nope. Casey and I were talking in the living room when we heard a crash. Someone threw a large rock through my windshield and redid my paint job."

"What?"

"They spray-painted the word 'bitch' across the back end of the truck," Casey explained as he joined them in the hall.

Layla motioned down the little hall. "Why don't we all go in the dining room and I'll get some sweet tea."

"Sounds like a *sweet* idea." Casey laughed and sauntered awkwardly toward the dining room.

"That pal of yours is quite the joker. I like him." Henry followed Casey, leaving Ben and Layla alone.

"I'm sorry my text upset you." She wrapped her arms around him and planted a kiss on his lips. "But, as you can see, I'm fine. Casey was here to protect me."

Yeah. Casey was there to protect her. I *should have been the one to protect her.* "Would you consider staying at my place until they figure out what's going on here?"

"You know I can't. I have Casey and my animals and what's left of my house to take care of."

"How long's he staying?" Ben nodded down the hall toward the voices filtering out of the dining room.

"As long as he wants. You keep asking me that.' She put her hands on her hips and studied him quietly. "Are you still jealous?"

He frowned at her. "No. Of course not."

She smiled in response. "Ben?"

"Okay. Fine. Maybe just a little." He stuck his hands in his pockets and offered her a small smile. "Shouldn't we get that tea?"

"The tea will wait. I told you before, Casey is just a friend. You didn't strike me as the jealous type."

"I'm not. Not usually. I've been all messed up the last couple days."

"You have *nothing* to worry about. I've known Casey since I was about six. If something were going to happen between us, it would have happened a long time ago. Besides, I'm not much of a Navy girl. I like a good, sharp airmen's uniform." She rubbed her hands up his arms slowly, licking her lips as she watched him for his reaction.

"I think I still have my dress blues. I can dig them out later." His voice had gone husky as he leaned toward her. "They might even still fit. I've only lost a few pounds."

Their lips met briefly, and then Layla pulled back. "I look forward to it," she whispered. "Let's get some tea now and go talk to Henry about what's going on."

CHAPTER FIFTEEN

Layla followed Ben from the kitchen to the dining room. He'd insisted on carrying the tray, so she'd let him. She found it adorable that he'd been so worried about her but worrisome that he still thought there was something with Casey to be jealous of.

"We were wondering if you two went off to get a little sweet tea of your own." Casey grinned and offered a fist bump to the police officer beside him.

"Casey!" She pretended to be angry and swatted him on the shoulder.

He grinned. "What? I don't ever remember it taking you twenty minutes to pour four glasses of tea."

Layla furrowed her brow in mock anger. "You

are... you're just... impossible."

"Yeah. You can't help but love me though. Rob said you have to. It was his last request."

She shook her head and sat down across the table from Casey. "What am I going to do with you?"

"So, I hate to interrupt all this lovely banter, but I need to get a little more information from Ms. Evans and get back out on the road," Henry cut in. "I know y'all think I don't have anything to do all day, but this county is full of criminal element."

"Criminal element?" Ben eyed the police officer. "Seriously?"

Henry laughed. "Okay, so this is the busiest I've been in five years, but still. I need to get a move on."

"We appreciate your efforts, sir," Casey said.

"I know I've asked before, but let me try one more time. Do you have any enemies that you know of? This latest attack definitely seems personal toward you."

"I've pissed a lot of people off over the last ten years," Layla replied.

"Anyone recently?"

She decided it was finally time to tell the cop what had been on her mind. "Pretty much all of Virginia Beach. My last big case, I let a child rapist and murderer go free."

"You did?" The disgust in the officer's voice was blatant as he shook his head.

Defense attorneys were notoriously not loved by cops, but she hadn't expected such an obvious reaction to her former career. "I defended him, like he had the right to. That's why I moved here—I couldn't live with myself anymore after that."

"I never understood why anyone would do defense. We work hard to get those bastards off the streets, and then some yahoo comes along and finds a technicality." Officer Blake scowled.

"The justice system allows for everyone to have a right to defend themselves in court. What about those people who really are innocent? Don't they deserve someone to stand up for them?"

"Is that what you did?" Henry asked. "Or were you just in it for the money?"

"Come on, Blake, don't you think you're being a little harsh?" Casey interjected. "She was doing her job. If she didn't defend her clients to the best of her ability, she wasn't doing what her oath demanded of her."

Blake held up his hands in mock surrender. "Sorry. I'm just a little touchy about criminals being allowed to get away. Anyway, if you can think of anything or anyone who might be responsible for what's been happening here, give me a call. I'll do the same if we get any leads."

He rose from the chair and nodded at Casey and Ben. To Layla, he handed his business card. "Thanks for the tea." His tone was still pretty cool but professional.

Layla accepted the card. "Thanks for looking into things. Sorry to have brought so much trouble to your town."

"I'll walk you out," Ben said as he led Henry from the room.

Layla stood by the door and listened to the two men as they walked away.

"I still can't believe your girl was on the wrong side of the bench."

"Give it a rest, Blake. She quit, didn't she? And besides, she doesn't deserve to have her property destroyed for being a lawyer."

"Legally, no. Morally, maybe she does deserve it."

Layla sucked in a breath and struggled to hold back her tears. The officer hated her because of a job she no longer did or cared to do.

"I'm not sure that's your place to say, Officer Blake." Ben's tone was considerably cooler. "It's your job to find the bad guy, not judge the victim."

"I know my job, son." Blake's voice was equally cool.

She heard the door open, then close. Turning to Casey, she cleared her throat. "Why does everyone hate me?"

"That's a bit dramatic, don't you think?" He wrapped his arms around her and held her close. "You're a good woman, and that cop knows it. He's just a little sensitive. Probably got his balls slapped by a defense attorney or something."

"I still believe everyone has the right to representation. I just don't want to be that person anymore. Moving here was supposed to be my chance to start over."

He patted her back before stepping away a little. "It'll be okay, baby girl. I promise."

The front door opened again, and Ben called out to them.

"We're still here in the dining room!" Layla called back.

Ben reappeared. "Blake's just an old codger. Nothing to worry about. He'll do his job. He just believes real strongly in the bad guy going to jail"

"So do I."

"Well, I'm in a bit of a pickle," Casey shoved his hands in his pockets and rocked back on his heels.

"I'm supposed to take a lady to a picnic, and you haven't got a truck anymore. I guess I'll give her a call."

Layla looked to Ben for help. If Casey didn't have his date, they wouldn't have any time alone, and what she really needed right then was some time in Ben's arms to forget about the mess that had become her life.

Ben must have read her mind. "I told you last night you could use my truck. She's a little temperamental, but she's sturdy. Or if you're up for a little fun, I might even have a better idea."

"What's that, man?" Casey sounded intrigued.

"Remember, I mentioned I've got an ATV in the barn?"

"Four wheels and mud tires?" Casey's excitement was obvious.

"Yup. You interested? It's a good way to get a good-looking woman's arms wrapped tight around you." Ben sent a smile in Layla's direction. "I plan to get Layla out there one of these days too."

Her entire body warmed at the thought of pressing against Ben's strong form as they flew over pastures and along the stream. She smiled at him. "Sounds good to me."

Casey nodded. "Yeah. That does sound pretty sweet. Thanks, man."

"Come on, I'll take you up to my place and you can ride her back. Get the feel of things before your lady friend gets here."

"You gonna be okay for a bit?" Casey asked her.

"Absolutely. I think I'll take a long hot bath." As far as she could tell, Casey was as excited about the big-boy toy he was about to ride as he was about the woman he would be riding with.

He leaned over and pressed a kiss to her cheek "You're the best. I'm gonna grab a jacket and I'll meet you out front, Marshall."

When he was gone, Layla turned to Ben. "Thank you. He needs that."

"What?"

"To be treated like a normal guy."

Ben smiled and traced the outline of her jaw with his thumb. "To be honest, I didn't really do it for him."

"You say that, but I know you've got a big heart."

"Okay, so maybe it was a little bit for him."

She leaned in, intending to place a quick kiss on his lips before sending him after Casey, but Ben had other ideas. He wrapped his strong arms around her and pulled her against his chest while his lips found hers. The kiss was quick but passionate, filled with promises of what was to come.

———

HE COULD STILL TASTE THE SWEET TEA THAT HAD BEEN on Layla's lips as he drove Casey back to his place. They had the windows down, and the fresh spring air saturated his nostrils with smells and scents he'd never noticed before.

Is this what it's like to be in love?

If so, what had he felt for Lauren, because it was nothing like what was happening to him now?

Casey sat in the passenger seat singing along to Billy Joel's "It's Still Rock and Roll to Me," and he sounded relaxed and happy. It had been less than a year since losing his leg, and the other man was in a much better place mentally than Ben had been a year after his time as a POW. His outlook on life was remarkable. It made Ben angry at himself for wasting so much time. Of course, if things had gone differently, he may not have ever met Layla, and that was worth all of it. It was absolutely amazing what she'd done for his heart and soul in just a few days.

"Here we are," Ben said as he pulled into the driveway. "Casa de Marshall."

Casey scanned the area. "Nice property you got here, man."

"Thanks. I like it. Got it for a steal too. The barn needs work, but nothing I can't get done over time."

"A little hard work never hurt a man."

"Nope," Ben agreed.

It took just a few minutes to get Casey used to the ATV. He rode circles around the driveway and then disappeared into the woods behind the house.

Ben pulled out his cell phone from his pants pocket and saw he'd missed a message from Layla.

How's Casey doing?

He typed back. **Casey's fine. Just took off on my ATV.**

Almost instantly a new text arrived.

I hope he doesn't get lost... oh, wait, you military guys can find your way out of anywhere with a piece of string and a Tic Tac... lol

He really did laugh out loud and again marveled at the sound. Ben was finally finding his way back to his old self, and it felt good.

Can't wait to spend some time with you today.

Layla replied, **Me too. Casey couldn't have shown up at a worse time. And I love him to death, you know. lol**

Lol! I know you do, but I couldn't help wishing a little that he had at least waited a day. His timing was... unfortunate... yesterday.

After he hit Send, he wondered if he shouldn't have mentioned that. Maybe she was glad Casey had interrupted them.

I almost punched him in the nose after I got over the excitement of seeing him.

Good! She was as disappointed as he was. That meant today might not be so awkward.

Another text came in.

I would have kept you at my place all night long.

After several deep breaths to calm his racing pulse, he messaged her back.

And I would have kept you awake all night long.

It was so long after he hit Send before she replied that he started to think he'd scared her off.

Then she replied, and he dropped his phone when he read what she wrote.

I'm naked.

Holy crap. Every cell in his body screamed at him to run all the way to her place,

but the hum of the ATV's engine reached his ears. *Damn it.* Casey was back. He picked up his phone and replied. **Stay that way. Casey just got back. As soon as he leaves with his date, I'll make it worth your while.**

She responded almost immediately. **I can't wait.**

The simple answer was more erotic than pretty much anything he'd ever heard. He stowed his phone and waved Casey over.

The other man pulled the ATV up beside Ben and grinned. "Wow. Are you really that happy to see me?"

"What?"

Casey nodded toward the front of Ben's cargos. The loose pants were very obviously tenting. His face heated, but he tried to play it cool. "Don't you know it? A man on a four-wheeler is downright sexy."

Casey grinned. "You talked to Layla while I was gone, didn't you?"

He frowned. "No." It wasn't a lie.

"Liar."

He held up his phone. "We didn't technically *talk*. *She* texted me. Did you enjoy your ride?"

"Not as much as you're going to enjoy yours this afternoon." Casey started laughing so hard he nearly tumbled off the four-wheeler.

Ben growled. "Were you always this obnoxious, or did you hit your head in your accident too?"

"Harsh, man." Casey passed him the one-finger salute.

Ben just laughed, returning the gesture. "You want to ride this back to Layla's place? I'll follow you in the truck."

With a big grin, Casey gunned the engine and spun the tires. "Race ya!" He was gone in a cloud of dust.

Ben ran to his truck, turned it on, and threw it in to gear, but when he got onto the road, the other man was nowhere to be seen.

Layla smiled at the phone in her hand. That was the closest she'd ever come to talking dirty to a man, and as mild as it was, it was fun. She wasn't really naked, but as soon as Casey left, she would be. All she'd dreamed about the night before was where things would have gone if Casey hadn't shown up when he did.

A knock sounded at the front door, and she ran for it thinking the boys were back. The house had been locked down like a fortress just to be on the safe side. Too bad she didn't think to look outside before she yanked the door open and found a shotgun pointed at her face.

"What… what are *you* doing here? How did you find me?"

The shotgun lowered and jabbed against her chest. "A very helpful girl answered the phone at your old office and wanted to make sure all your mail got forwarded to the correct address."

"Are you the one…?"

"That barn sure went up fast, huh? Too bad your do-gooder boyfriend ran in after you. We could have avoided this very unpleasant meeting." Her visitor jabbed her with the barrel of the gun again. "Let's go."

She shook her head. "I'm not going anywhere with you."

"That's a damn shame for your buddy with the fake leg."

"Casey? What did you do to Casey?" She tried to stay as calm as she could, but her voice turned shrill, giving away her mounting fear.

"ATVs shouldn't ride on county roads, you know. Accidents happen."

She lunged at him. "Accidents? You son of a bitch, you better not have hurt him!"

He waved the shotgun toward the woods behind the house. "I'm pretty sure he's gonna be all right as long as we get him some help. You come with me, I'll call 9-1-1 and send rescuers to him."

She looked past the intruder and saw no vehicle in the yard. "Where are we going?"

He narrowed his eyes and tapped his foot impatiently. "You'll find out once we get there. Now, we going or what?"

"How did you hit Casey without a vehicle?" Maybe if she kept talking, Ben would show up.

"I never said I hit him. You talk too much." He waved a cell phone. "What's it gonna be? I shoot you here and now and your buddy dies alone in the woods, or go with me and I call for help for him."

She had no choice. Casey had survived too much to die alone in the woods somewhere. She had no idea what had happened to him or how badly he was hurt. This was her problem, and he didn't deserve to pay the price. "Fine, I'll go. But call first."

"No." He shoved her shoulder with the weapon. "We walk first."

He motioned for her to step outside, and she complied. Layla didn't close the door behind her. With any luck, Ben would see it that way, know something was wrong, and call for help.

"Fine. Where are we going?"

"Just walk. That way." He pushed her shoulder blade with his shotgun, and she stumbled.

They were headed in the direction of the wood

line on the north side of the house. Once they went in there, Ben would never find them. She dragged her feet in the dirt, trying to leave scuff marks that someone might notice. At least then they would know which way she'd been taken.

When they disappeared into the tree line, Layla stopped walking. "Call EMS now."

He laughed with no humor. "You don't get to be in charge this time, my dear. I do."

She crossed her arms over her chest. "You said if I went with you, you would get Casey help."

"How does it feel to be helpless to save someone you love?"

She whirled around to face her captor. "You have no idea how sorry I am, Mr. Owens, but this is not the way to get justice for Cecilia."

"No." Derek Owens scowled and ran a hand through his already wild hair. "It's not, but at least you'll understand what you did was wrong. Now turn around and walk."

He jabbed her with the gun in her gut so hard it made her double over. "The man had a right to a defense," she gasped.

"And my daughter had the right to grow up."

His words sliced right through her heart. He had no idea how she'd agonized over that case. Layla caught her breath and stood up straight. Derek started pushing her along again. They didn't speak for a good ten minutes until they stepped into a clearing with a little shack right in the center of it.

"Where are we?"

He feigned shock. "What? You don't know your property? This is an old shack for ranch hands and cowboys spending the night out with the cattle while working. It's quite cozy actually."

Smoke spiraled slowly from the old stone chimney and a light shone through the only window. "You've made yourself comfortable, I see."

Derek shrugged. "I did what I had to do."

"Did you enjoy burning down my barn and defacing my cows?"

"Immensely. I thought I would give you a little of the uncertainty that my wife and I experienced when Cecilia disappeared." Derek reached past her and pushed open the door to the shack. "Inside. Now."

She did as she was told, entering the small space. Derek forced her over to a rickety old chair. "Sit."

"That's not going to hold me." As soon as she sat down, Derek would incapacitate her and she'd be done. No chance to escape.

"It'll hold. Now sit."

Something in the man's voice told her not to argue anymore. The chair creaked but held her weight as Derek secured her wrists and ankles to the back and legs with a piece of old rope.

"None of this will bring Cecilia back." Layla tried to keep her muscles flexed as he bound her so that when she relaxed, the ties would be looser. It was all she could think of at the moment to help her situation. It wasn't nearly enough.

Derek shrugged. "Nope, I don't expect it will. But you get to sit here for a while and wonder where your friend is and start to panic that he might not be alive, and I get to watch. Eventually I'll kill you, and it'll make me feel a whole lot better about you letting that man go free. Or maybe when you're dead, I'll go back and kill your boyfriend too. Even better, I think I'll go do it now. Let you think about living without him for a while."

He cracked open the shotgun, checked it for shells, and then clicked it closed before heading toward the door.

"Wait!" Layla called after him. "You killed him, didn't you?"

Derek smiled, his expression remaining cold. "He never should have left the courthouse that day."

Desperation set in. "He had a fair trial in front of

a jury of his peers. I just did the job I was sworn to do. I didn't *want* him to go free!"

"I highly doubt that." He scowled. "You liked your fancy car and fancy condo and fancy life way too much not to win such a high-profile case."

"But I gave it all up after that case. Moved here and gave up practicing law. Cecilia's death was an awful tragedy, but I wasn't the one that killed her. You have to stop blaming me." She lowered her voice. "Why don't you just let me go and head back to Virginia Beach? I won't tell anyone I saw you."

He shook his head. "Nah. I don't think so. Enjoy your afternoon. I promise I'll put him down slowly and painfully. Just the way he likes it."

The door to the little shack slammed shut, leaving Layla alone with her panic. The echo of his laughter filtered through the various cracks in the plank wall. She let out a sob of fear and frustration. First he hurt Casey and now he wanted to hurt Ben. She had to get out of there.

Derek Owens was going after Ben. He may have already killed Casey, and now he was going back for the one man in this world she thought she could actually love. Hot tears filled her eyes, but she held them back. Crying wasn't about to do her any good.

She tugged at the bonds on her wrists and ankles.

The echo of Owens' promise filled her mind: *"I promise I'll put him down slowly and painfully. Just the way he likes it."*

Does that horrible man know about Ben's past?

How could he?

Everything was such a mess. Moving away was supposed to fix everything for everyone. Apparently Derek hadn't gotten the memo on that.

Ben had already had his share of pain. Layla struggled against her bonds. She had to get to Ben. There was no way she could let him go through torture a second time in his life. Especially not when it was all her fault Derek had even come there.

LAYLA'S DRIVEWAY WAS EMPTY, AND THE AIR FELT TOO still. Little hairs at the base of his neck stood at attention, his warning system that all was not right.

Something was, in fact, very, very wrong.

Casey was nowhere in sight, and the front door to Layla's place was wide open. He'd made her promise to keep it closed and locked at all times; no way she would have just left it open like that. His gut told him something bad had happened. He jumped from the truck and ran to her house. Resisting the urge to call after her, Ben let his training take over, and he slowly entered the darkened house. He knew the second he crossed the threshold that she wasn't there, but he checked every room anyway.

When he reached her bedroom, Ben paused in the doorway, remembering the one time he'd been in that room the day before. Breathing deep, he absorbed the smell that was so distinctly Layla, letting it fuel his adrenaline. God help the person who harmed a single hair on her head.

Slipping back through the house, he stepped out onto the porch and looked around slowly, paying careful attention to every little detail. Off to the side, he noticed a series of drag marks in the dirt.

Jumping off the porch without using the steps, Ben got down on one knee and

examined the marks. He could make out the imprint of what looked like the sole of a pair of work boots. The other marks could have been from a pair of tennis shoes. Every so often, there was a chevron print in the dirt that was typical of athletic shoes. Following the marks slowly, he stopped when they reached grass at the edge of the wood line and let his years of training take over again, looking for signs that someone had passed through the area.

Blades of grass were trampled, a broken, still

green stick hung from a tree, and the brush had been flattened to make a path in the wooded area. Someone had been there. More than once. He listened to the sounds of nature. Birds chirped, a few cicadas were enjoying the warmer, late spring weather, and high above him several crows flew in a circle.

Crows were scavengers. They circled dead and dying animals, waiting to feast on their flesh. Panic gripped him in its steel grasp, and everything he knew about sneaking up on the enemy nearly left him as he fought the urge to run through the woods screaming for Layla.

Instead he picked his way along the fresh trail, looking for any signs that someone had come that way earlier that morning. A few hundred feet in, it became very obvious that this was a well-traveled path. Ben got the feeling that this was the way Layla's stalker had been accessing her property for some time. How many times? Had he been watching her long before the destruction of her property had begun?

Off in the distance, he heard a siren that grew louder quickly. Stopping for a second, he listened to the sound of the police car. It got so loud that it nearly drowned out the sound of the shotgun being shucked behind him.

"Don't move," a gruff voice commanded.

Ben lifted his hands slightly and started to turn around. "Hey, man, I don't want any trouble."

"I *said* don't move!" The voice was louder this time as the barrel of the shotgun the man held jabbed him hard between the shoulder blades.

"I'm not moving. I told you, I don't want any trouble."

"You may not want it, buddy, but trouble has found you. Start walking."

Another sharp jab of the gun barrel sent a sharp pain down his spine as Ben tripped forward.

"What's this all about?" he asked as he made his way back the way he had come. The sound of the sirens had gone faint again as the car passed by Layla's place and kept on going.

"Your little girlfriend, of course."

"What do you know about her? Who *are* you?"

"A blast from her past." The man laughed, making a weird cackling noise before he dissolved into a fit of coughing that actually forced him to stop walking as he hacked so hard he vomited.

"You all right, man?" He wasn't sure he actually

cared. His need to find Layla grew with every footstep.

"I'm fine," he growled.

Ben turned slightly to look at the man over his shoulder and caught sight of red streaks on the thin white cloth he wiped his mouth with. His captor was bent over, his skin a very pale shade of blue.

"You don't sound fine. I've got a bit of medical training. I can help."

The man stood up and scowled. "I don't need your help. What I *need* is justice for my little girl. Now start walking!"

They continued along the path back toward Layla's house in silence. Ben used the time to figure out how to get away from the man without getting shot in the back with a twelve-gauge slug. The man said he was from Layla's past and that he wanted justice for his little girl. It had to be that case that haunted her. The one that had driven her here from her home to try and escape.

"I'm not sure what your plan is, pal, but nothing is going to bring your little girl back."

"You think I don't know that?" The comment earned Ben another jab in the shoulder blade. "But Little Miss Defense Attorney needs to understand the pain and the loss my wife and I have lived with since our baby girl was taken from us. She set the bastard free! So now I'll show her what it feels like to lose someone she loves. Two someones, actually."

"What did you do to Casey?" They stepped out of the wood line beside Layla's house.

"Casey? Not to worry, that young man won't be interfering with your plays on Ms. Evans anymore." The man cackled. "Not that you will have any more plays when I'm through here."

"What did you do to him?" Ben demanded. How did the other man know anything about his envy over Casey and Layla's relationship anyway? "Have you been spying on us?"

"It was so easy. You and attorney girl just go at it wherever you want to—lips and tongues and hands everywhere. In my day, a lady played a little hard to get."

"You don't know anything about Layla, so I suggest you not say anymore." They'd reached the front steps. The door was still open, and the shotgun steered him inside.

"Oh, I know plenty. I know she thinks nothing of selling out her conscience for a good chunk of change. She has no trouble sleeping after letting the rapist and murderer of a little girl free and making it so he can never be charged with the crime again. I also know she doesn't have any family nearby, and with her one-legged friend and you out of the picture, no one will even miss her. Not until I'm long gone anyway." He broke into another coughing fit as he motioned with the gun. "Now, get over there and sit in that chair," the man rasped between coughs.

"I don't think so. Where's Layla?"

"Somewhere nearby wondering if you're dead or alive or somewhere in between. Now, do what I say."

Ben wasn't going down without a fight. No freaking way. As they crossed the open living area, he stopped suddenly and turned, his arm shooting out and grabbing for the gun barrel.

"Not so fast, mister!" the man yelled, cracking him on the top of the head with the wood stock of the gun.

Sounds faded, lights dimmed, and Ben went down with a crash onto the wood floor.

———

BEN HAD NO IDEA HOW MUCH TIME HAD PASSED WHEN he came to, sitting in a chair with his hands bound behind his back. His head ached and his vision was blurry. Squeezing his eyes shut, he counted to three in his head and then opened them slowly. Things were slightly clearer but not by much.

"You're finally awake."

"What the hell did you hit me with? A damn sledgehammer?"

"Just ole' Jimmy here." He raised the butt of his shotgun and let out a dry laugh that quickly turned to another round of hacking.

"Man, you need to get to a hospital or something."

The man shook his head. "Ain't nothing they can do for me. I'm terminal, the doc says. Got nothing to lose here now."

"Where's Layla?"

"Come now, Miss Defense Attorney will be just fine. At least until I'm done here." He pulled out a hunting knife. The mother-of-pearl handle glinted in the sunlight coming in the window. "See this here blade? I just had her sharpened last week."

Ben tried hard to remain calm. Number one rule was never let the enemy see they were getting to you. Little beads of sweat still broke out on his forehead as his captor moved closer, flipping the knife around in his fingers. Fear churned in Ben's gut.

He had to keep his head on straight. If he could

keep the man talking, maybe he could figure out a plan. "What's your name?"

"Doesn't matter." He drew the knife slowly across the arm of Ben's shirt. It wasn't enough pressure to slice through flesh, but it left a cut in the fabric. He jerked his arm and the man cackled.

"We're going to have so much fun." The man ran the tip of the blade from Ben's left shoulder and across his chest, landing just in front of his kidneys. The sting of the steel as it hit his skin through the fabric was painful, but he bit down against it.

"You are one sick bastard."

"What? You don't like my little game?" He waved his knife in front of Ben's face, getting dangerously close. "I thought you enjoyed this sort of thing."

Ben ground his molars together to avoid responding. The man was trying to goad him, and he refused to fall into the trap.

"I've been watching the two of you. I know about your time as a POW. That must have been awful." He lightly pulled the blade across Ben's thigh.

"Like I said, you are one sick bastard."

"You know what would have been even better? I should have brought Ms. Evans here to *watch* instead of making her wonder. Of course, my wife and I had to wonder. For forty-eight excruciating hours, we had to sit and imagine what our little Cecilia was going through. Guess what? Our imaginations weren't good enough. He did things to her that I couldn't even fathom. That's the sick bastard, sir. The one who had the high-paid, high-powered, low-moral defense attorney. How did she live with herself defending a person like that?"

Ben held his gaze, refusing to back down.

The man raised the knife to Ben's throat and looked him deep in the eyes, pressing the blade against his carotid artery. "Tell me. How does she do it?"

"I don't," Layla called from the door.

CHAPTER SEVENTEEN

DEREK SWUNG AROUND TO LOOK AT HER. THE KNIFE clattered against the wood flooring as he yanked his shotgun from the table. Layla sucked in a breath and grabbed the baseball bat she kept in the umbrella stand by the door. Thank God Derek hadn't noticed it. Or maybe he didn't care since he expected her to be tied up in that rat-infested shack in the woods. The wood bat was no match for a shotgun—she wished she had her own gun—but it was something, and she intended to use it. No way would Ben have to endure another second of the misery she was responsible for. She would go down fighting for them both. It was about damned time she fought for the right things for a change.

"How did you get here?" Derek demanded.

"Derek, I am so sorry about Cecilia. And no one is sorrier about her killer going free than I am. Why do you think I gave up law? Moved myself to the middle of nowhere? Because I *couldn't* live with myself, and I didn't want to ever hurt another family again the way I did yours."

"Too little, too late." Derek stepped a bit closer, his shotgun pointed at her chest again.

"How many times do I have to tell you? Everyone is allowed the right to counsel. Everyone, no matter how horrible they are, has the right to defend themselves. If it had been someone else working that case, he still would have gotten off. The evidence just wasn't there to meet the burden."

"'Burden'? Do you want to talk about burdens? My wife still cries herself to sleep every night. She hasn't left the house since the verdict. I'm about to die myself. Who's gonna take care of her when I'm gone? She needs peace, and this will give it to her."

"How? How will sitting through another murder trial do anything for her?" Layla held the bat to her shoulder and kept one eye on the barrel of the gun that kept inching closer.

Beyond Derek's shoulder, she could see Ben. He'd already worked his hands free of the ropes that bound him and now attempted to untie his legs. He caught her eye and nodded slightly. She had to keep Derek talking until Ben was able to get totally free.

"I'll be dead in a month. The cancer got me, you know. There won't be a trial. I'll plead guilty and let the state pay my medical care."

Layla glanced again past Derek and saw that Ben had freed one leg and was working on the second.

Unfortunately, Derek caught her action. "What you looking at, girlie?" he demanded, spinning around.

"Look out, Ben!"

Layla lunged at Derek just as the shotgun went off. The explosion was deafening as wood splintered and glass shattered.

Layla screamed. She raised the bat and brought it down on Derek, missing his skull but slamming into the shoulder that his shotgun rested against. The man let out an agonizing wail as he turned the gun back on her. Ben lay sprawled on the ground, one leg still tied to the chair. As she raised the bat once more, Derek fired off another shell that narrowly missed her head. Swinging low with the bat, she nailed him in the kneecaps, and the man crashed to the floor, the shotgun flying from his hands. It hit the floor and slid down the hall.

Derek let out a string of curses as he tried to drag himself toward the gun.

"Oh no you don't!" Ben jumped up to his knees, dragging the chair behind

him, and gave the man a chop to the back of the head with the side of his hand. Derek dropped to the floor with a thump.

"Ben!" Layla ran to him, falling to her knees and knocking Ben to the floor again. "I thought he shot you!"

"I've got great reflexes. Jumped out of the way just in time," he replied, then crushed his lips against hers. His hands were everywhere on her body, trying to assess injuries as much as he was desperate to touch her.

He rolled her over so he could look deep into her eyes. "I thought I'd lost you."

"I'm so sorry, Ben. I never meant to involve you in my troubles. I thought if I left the city, just disappeared, the Owenses would be able to mourn and get past it all. Obviously I was wrong."

She squeezed her eyes closed against the hot tears that now flowed uncontrollably.

Ben kissed first one eyelid, then the other. "I've been in worse situations."

"I know! And now—"

"And now the two of you are going to finally go get a room, right?" a familiar voice called from the front porch.

"Casey!" Layla cried, jumping to her feet and running to her friend. "He said you were dead!"

"Oh please, I've jumped from planes and choppers into enemy territory. Even an explosive couldn't take me out. A little four-wheeler accident isn't nearly enough to take me out permanently." Casey's limp was worse, and there was blood on his head and shirt, but he was alive.

To Ben he said, "Good thinking having the go bag on the ATV."

Ben freed his other leg from the wood chair. "Always prepared for anything, right, man?"

"I called 9-1-1. That cop friend of yours ought to be here any minute."

As if on cue, a siren sounded in the distance, and in no time at all, Henry Blake

stood in the door. "What the hell happened here?"

"This is the guy who's been stalking me this week." Layla pointed to the heap that was Derek still passed out on the floor. "He tried to kill Casey, kidnapped me, and was about to kill Ben when I found them. He's not dead, just knocked out. But I did give him a couple extra whacks, just to be sure."

The words left her in a jumble. The adrenaline rush that had been coursing through her veins began to crash, and her whole body shook.

Ben stepped up and put an arm across her shoulders. "Let's go sit down."

She nodded and let him lead her to the sofa. As she lowered herself to the seat, the room began to sway a bit around her. "Ben, I don't feel so well—"

———

THE ROOM WAS DARK WHEN LAYLA OPENED HER EYES again. She glanced around, trying to get her bearings while her eyes adjusted. She was in her bedroom; the familiar shapes of her furniture slowly came into focus, as did the scents that were uniquely hers. Her head ached, and her muscles felt tense.

The soft sound of someone breathing in the darkness sent her heart racing as she tried to find something she could use as a weapon. What had Derek Owens done to her while she was unconscious? It didn't matter. He wasn't going to do anything else. She would go down fighting.

"Layla?" a voice asked softly in the dark. "Are you awake?"

Ben.

"Yes," she replied, her own voice shaky. She felt the bed shift as someone sat down beside her.

"How are you feeling?" He gently rubbed her hair back from her forehead, his touch so tender it almost made her heart ache.

"What happened?"

"You fainted. Too much adrenaline."

She suddenly remembered the fight. Derek shooting, Ben hitting the floor, that ridiculous knife Derek had used to cut Ben. She shot upright in the bed and crushed him to her. "Are you okay, Ben? I'm sorry. I'm so sorry he hurt you because of me!"

He kissed the top of her head and rubbed her back in soft, even circles. "I'm fine, Layla. Really. It takes so much more than that to take me out of the picture."

Casey had said the same thing.

Casey!

"Where's Casey? Is he okay?"

Ben chuckled. "I'd say right about now, he is way more than okay. Stacy showed up right after you passed out. She took him to the hospital to get checked out. He called an hour ago. He's going to be busy for the better part of the evening."

"Oh, good. I couldn't stand to lose him too. I lose everyone who loves me."

"Not everyone," Ben whispered against her ear. "You're never going to lose me. I promise. Thank you for saving me."

"I didn't save you. You knocked Derek out with some crazy samurai move."

He sat back a little and looked at her. Even in the dark, Layla could see how sharp and clear his blue eyes were. "No, I mean thank you for saving me from myself. Before you came into my life, I was a tormented man being eaten alive from the inside out. You saved me, Layla, and I want to spend the rest of my days thanking you for it. Starting right now." He wrapped his arms around her.

"Wait." She pushed him away. "I need to thank you too."

"For what?" Ben looked confused.

"When I moved here, I was running away. I told myself I was doing the right thing, making up for my horrendous mistakes, but what I was really doing was hiding. I could no longer face myself and what I had become."

"I'm sure you weren't the monster you thought you were." Ben picked up her hand and kissed her fingers.

"I was, Ben. Money was my motivator—fortune and status. I liked being feared in court. It gave me power, and I really liked power. The better I got, the more people wanted me, and those high-profile cases started falling in my lap. After a while, nothing else mattered. You changed all that."

"I don't know about that. I'm pretty messed up myself."

"When I thought of you here, alone with that madman, I couldn't get out of that cabin fast enough. I was so afraid he would hurt you, the way those other men had. He seemed hell-bent on causing you pain to hurt me."

"I love that you wanted to save me." Still holding her hand, Ben turned it over and pressed a kiss to the inside of her wrist. Trailing more kisses up her arm, he pulled her close and wrapped his arms around her.

She pressed her palm to his cheek, covering the scar with her touch. "You've already endured so much. I couldn't let you go through that too."

"Maybe it's time we both let go of our demons," he whispered, his breath warm and tantalizing against her ear.

Layla nodded as a single tear escaped one eye. "Seems to me like maybe we need each other."

"I think maybe we do," he whispered before his lips burned a path from her earlobe, along her jawline, over her shoulder, and down to the hollow at the base of her neck. Her hands followed the same path across Ben's shoulders and chest. She only then noticed that he wasn't wearing a shirt. "Are you already undressed?"

"My shirt was torn," he replied as he slowly lowered her against the pillows, his fingers continuing the exploration of her torso his lips had begun. Layla ran her fingertips across Ben's chest, feeling every raised line and mark. She expected him to pull back from her touch, but instead it only seemed to fuel the urgency of his kisses.

She ran her hands up the chiseled muscles of his back and shoulders, loving the feel of it.

Breaking their kiss, he looked down at her, his blue eyes dark with deep emotion.

"Layla," he whispered against her lips, "I think I've fallen in love you."

"I know exactly what you mean," she whispered back. "Now, don't just tell me, show me."

I HOPE YOU LOVED BEN AND LAYLA'S STORY. IF YOU'RE new to the Marshall brothers, be sure to check out MURDER ON THE MOUNTAIN and BLUE RIDGE

Murder, the other stand-alone romances in this series.

I appreciate your help in spreading the word, including telling a friend. Before you go, it would mean so much to me if you would take a few minutes to write a review and share how you feel about my story so others may find my work. Reviews really do help readers find books. Please leave a review on your favorite book site.

Be sure to also join my newsletter to receive all the news first: Join my newsletter: WWW.CAROLYN-LAROCHE.WORDPRESS.COM

ACKNOWLEDGMENTS

I want to thank the amazing team at Hot Tree Publishing and Hot Tree Editing for helping me make this story amazing. It's been a work in progress for a long time and the final product is all I could have ever hoped for and more. Ben is the Marshall brother that tugged at all my heartstrings, and he deserves a story that shows that.

BookSmith designs—you knocked another cover out of the park. Thank you for such a beautiful work of art!

To my readers, thank you a thousand times for your support! Books are journeys whose stories remain a mystery until the pages are turned. I love and appreciate everyone that taken those trips.

If not for the support of my family, I wouldn't be

where I am in my writing career. Thank you to my husband and my boys. Also, Allie, the editor that picked out my manuscript from the slush pile all those years ago and gave me my first step into traditional publishing. We are very good friends and often joke that we share part of the same brain! Sometimes we truly wonder if this is the case!

ABOUT THE AUTHOR

Science teacher by day, writer and baseball mom by night, Carolyn LaRoche lives near the ocean with her husband, two boys, rescue puppy, and four cats She loves crocheting, books, food videos and trying new recipes.

Join my newsletter:

WWW.CAROLYNLAROCHE.WORDPRESS.COM

I'd love to hear from you directly, too. Please feel free to email me at CAROLYNLAROCHEAUTHOR@YAHOO.COM or check out my website WWW.CAROLYNLAROCHE.WORDPRESS.COM for updates.

facebook.com/CarolynLaRocheAuthor

twitter.com/CarolynLaRoche

instagram.com/CarolynLaRocheAuthor

bookbub.com/authors/carolyn-laroche

ABOUT THE PUBLISHER

Hot Tree Publishing opened its doors in 2015 with an aspiration to bring quality fiction to the world of readers. With the initial focus on romance and a wide spread of romance subgenres, Hot Tree Publishing has since opened their first imprint, Tangled Tree Publishing, specializing in crime, mystery, suspense, and thriller.

Firmly seated in the industry as a leading editing provider to independent authors and small publishing houses, Hot Tree Publishing is the sister company to Hot Tree Editing, founded in 2012. Having established in-house editing and promotions, plus having a well-respected market presence, Hot Tree Publishing endeavors to be a leader in bringing quality stories to the world of readers.

Interested in discovering more amazing reads brought to you by Hot Tree Publishing? Head over to the website for information:

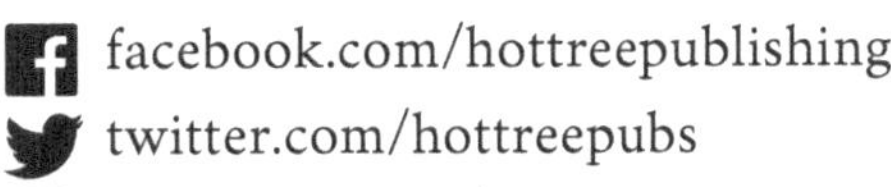 facebook.com/hottreepublishing
twitter.com/hottreepubs
instagram.com/hottreepublishing